Praise

"Hoffmann...
of this s..... ....ded conclusion."
—*RT Book Reviews* on *The Mighty Quinns: Dex*

"Keep your fan handy! It was impossible for me
to put this steamy, sexy book down until the
last page was turned."
—*Fresh Fiction* on *The Mighty Quinns: Jack*

"Strong, imperfect but lovable characters,
an interesting setting and great sensuality."
—*RT Book Reviews* on *The Mighty Quinns: Brody*

"This is a fast read that is hard to tear the eyes from.
Once I picked it up I couldn't put it down."
—*Fresh Fiction* on *The Mighty Quinns: Dermot*

"Sexy, heartwarming and romantic, this is a story to
settle down with and enjoy—and then reread."
—*RT Book Reviews* on *The Mighty Quinns: Teague*

"The only drawback to this story is that it's far too short"!
—*Fresh Fiction* on *The Mighty Quinns: Kellan*

Dear Reader,

Welcome to another Mighty Quinn adventure! This time, we're introducing you to another branch of the family—the New Zealand Quinns: Malcolm, twins Rogan and Ryan, and Dana.

Rugged New Zealand is the perfect playground for these Quinns. Together they run an adventure travel business, giving vacationers the time of their lives all over the world. Adventure is in the Quinns' blood—their father is a legend in the climbing world, even years after his untimely death on an expedition. Malcolm, as the eldest, has taken responsibility for the business and for his siblings. So when his father's body is discovered and reporters swarm the family, Mal is determined to protect his mother and siblings from going through that pain again.

Amy Engalls is equally determined to get an interview from Mal. She's staked her career on this story, and she won't leave New Zealand empty-handed. But Mal has no intention of letting Amy leave just yet. He promises her an adventure...and not just on the mountain. It's not the story she came for, it's not the experience she expected to have, but together, she and Mal may just find ecstasy...and love.

Enjoy the trip!

The Editors

Kate Hoffmann

—

The Mighty Quinns: Malcolm

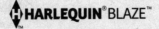

Recycling programs
for this product may
not exist in your area.

ISBN-13: 978-0-373-79798-1

THE MIGHTY QUINNS: MALCOLM

Copyright © 2014 by Peggy A. Hoffmann

Printed in U.S.A.

ABOUT THE AUTHOR

Kate Hoffmann began writing for Harlequin in 1993. Since then, she's published nearly eighty books, primarily in the Harlequin Temptation and Harlequin Blaze lines. When she isn't writing, she enjoys music, theater and musical theater. She is active working with high school students in the performing arts. She lives in southeastern Wisconsin with her cat, Chloe.

Books by Kate Hoffmann

HARLEQUIN BLAZE

HARLEQUIN SINGLE TITLES

Prologue

TENSION HUNG IN the air in the small house in Rotorua, setting everyone on edge. Ten-year-old Malcolm Quinn tried to keep his younger siblings occupied, seeing the growing worry in his mother's expression. But the twins, seven-year-olds Rogan and Ryan, knew something was up. Only their little sister, Dana, was unaware that all was not right.

Their father, Maxwell Quinn, had left advance base camp with his climbing party and Sherpas earlier that day, ready to conquer Everest. It was his father's sixth summit attempt and once complete, it would give him a perfect record.

Max Quinn and his partner, Roger Innis, had been guiding Everest expeditions for almost as long as Malcolm had been alive, first working for other expedition companies, and then for the past four seasons, working for themselves. Since founding Outbound Adventure, his father had rarely been home. But when he did walk through the front door, life was suddenly much brighter for the family. For in that moment, they all knew he was safe. They couldn't say that today.

"What time is it?" Rogan asked.

Mal looked up. His gaze met his brother's and Mal forced a smile. "Don't worry. They're probably just too busy to call. Or maybe they can't get through. Satellite telephones can be dodgy."

"But it's getting late," Ryan said. "It's nearly midnight. That means it's ten there. He should be back at camp by now, shouldn't he?"

"I'm sure he is. But he has a lot of responsibilities." Mal repeated the words that his mother had said to him just ten minutes before, hoping they calmed his brother's concern more than they had his.

Ryan rubbed his eyes. "What if something bad happened?"

"Yeah," Rogan said. "Maybe they're afraid to call us."

Mal crossed the room and pulled them both to their feet. "Go to bed. I'll wake you when the call comes. I promise."

To his great relief, they wandered off in the direction of their bedroom. Mal waited until the door shut behind them, then turned and hurried into the kitchen. Lydie Quinn sat at the kitchen table, Dana curled up in her arms, sound asleep. His mother was humming a tune that Mal didn't recognize, repeating the same phrase over and over again.

Mal silently walked by her and put the teakettle on to boil. When he sat down across from her, she refused to look at him, her eyes fixed on a point above his head.

"Mum?"

Her gaze didn't falter and the tune continued.

"Mum, would you like a cup of tea?"

Mal watched as tears welled up in his mother's eyes. He rose to comfort her and as he did, the phone rang.

"Don't answer it," she said.

"But, I—"

"Don't." She shook her head, the tears now tumbling down her cheeks. He'd never seen his mother cry before and Mal wasn't quite sure what to do. Dana stirred in her arms and Lydie grasped her daughter to her more tightly, rocking back and forth.

Mal quietly picked up the phone. "Hello?"

"Who is this?"

"Malcolm Quinn."

"Malcolm, it's Roger Innis. I need to speak with your mother."

"No," Malcolm said. "You can tell me."

"Son, put your mother on the phone. It's very important. This is no time for childish games."

"She won't speak with you," Mal insisted. "She can't. We know something is wrong. Just tell me and I'll tell her."

As he listened to his father's partner explain the situation, Mal slowly began to realize that his life—and the lives of his mother and siblings—would never be the same.

1

IT WAS GOOD to be home.

Malcolm Quinn grabbed his duffel from the back of his battered Range Rover and hefted it over his shoulder with a groan. He'd left Greenland three days ago after leading a four-week expedition across the ice cap from east to west, following the Arctic Circle. After boarding a bush flight from Greenland to Iceland, he'd flown from Reykjavik to Copenhagen, then to Dubai, then to Sydney and finally landed in Auckland just that morning after two days in airports. The two-hour drive home to Raglan was the final leg of his trip, and now that he was home, he could finally relax.

To say he was knackered was an understatement. But it was the good kind of exhaustion that he only experienced after a successful expedition. His clients had been thrilled with the experience and were grateful he'd led them on a trip without a single serious hitch.

But it was nice to be able to walk around in a light jacket and shorts. It was early April, spring in the northern hemisphere. But in New Zealand, winter was on its way. Still, the weather felt balmy compared to the constant cold of the Arctic.

The offices for Maximum Adrenaline were located in a low-slung white clapboard building just outside the town limits. For a company that specialized in high adventure, the office was rather unremarkable, distinguished from other nearby businesses by just a small sign above the door. A porch spanned the front facade; weathered wooden furniture was scattered along the wide expanse.

As he slammed the hatch on the SUV, the front door opened and the family dog, Duffy, came bounding out, followed by Mal's younger sister, Dana. "Hey, Duff, look at you. Hey, Dana."

The black Lab was so excited he wasn't sure what to do with himself, and when Mal squatted down, Duffy knocked him off his feet. He surrendered to a thorough tongue bath, laughing as the dog pinned him to the ground. When he finally was able to sit up, Duffy had stretched out across his lap, the dog's subtle way of keeping him in one spot.

"I can't move," Mal said to his sister, "or I'd give you a hug."

"Welcome home," Dana said. "I expected you tomorrow."

"I caught an earlier flight. Martin stayed with our gear to get it through customs. God, it's good to be home."

Duffy wriggled in his lap, nuzzling his wet nose under Mal's chin. "Enough, Duff," he said, struggling to his feet.

"He's missed you," Dana said.

"I'm sure he hasn't thought of me since I left. Considering the way you baby him, you're the only one he'd truly miss."

"I've been taking him running every day. And he's actually lost a bit of weight."

Mal bent down and patted the dog on his flank. "Ugh, don't talk about exercise. Right now, I need a stiff drink and a shower. And I'm not sure which I'll have first. Then, I'm heading into town to kick back and get laid. And I'm not sure which will come first."

It was an unwritten rule in the guiding business that you didn't bonk the clients, no matter how attractive they might be. He had one job and one job only—to bring his clients home safely. Sex was a distraction from that responsibility, especially in extreme environments. He was also a bit superstitious. You didn't disrespect the mountain gods.

That didn't mean the trekkers and climbers didn't have sex in their own tents, but Mal turned a blind eye and often made excuses when the locals were offended.

So from the time he left until the time he returned, he lived a celibate life. But when he got back to Raglan, Mal knew a handful of girls that were willing to provide a randy bloke with a night or two in bed, no strings attached. Raglan was a surf capital, a beach town with a plethora of pretty girls.

Though Mal and his brothers were considered attractive, there weren't many women on the North Island who wanted to settle down with a guy who was gone ten months out of the year, no matter how good he was in the sack. Which was just fine by Mal. He'd never been interested in anything long-term. His life was pretty perfect the way it was. And he wasn't prepared to alter it to make a woman happy—no matter how good *she* might be in bed.

Besides, he had his family's business to keep afloat. Any time wasted on a woman was time he could put to better use building their clientele, getting publicity for Maximum Adrenaline and working out new trips to offer.

"Any important messages for me?" Mal asked his sister as he got up.

He strode toward the door, but Dana stayed glued to the spot at the base of the porch steps. Mal turned to motion to her, then saw the pained expression on her face. A sick fear clutched at his gut and he drew a sharp breath. Something was wrong. "What is it? Is it Ryan? Rogan?"

His younger brother was climbing Lhotse in the Himalayas with an Aussie film crew. And Ryan's twin, Rogan, was in Alaska, doing a prep course for a Denali climb. Either trip had the potential for trouble. And then there were the other hundred or so guides that they employed on various expeditions throughout the year. "Who is it?"

"It's Dad," she murmured.

"Dad?" Their father had died twenty years ago this spring, somewhere near the summit of Mt. Everest. Mal had been ten, the twins seven and Dana only five.

His sister nodded, fighting back tears. "They found his body."

Mal gasped. "When?"

"Three weeks ago. Gary Branbauer's expedition. The snow cover has been light this year and as they were descending, they noticed a flash of color in the snow. It was him."

"How do they know?" Mal asked.

"They took a photo and got a GPS bearing. Roger Innis confirmed it was the right location and gear. The news is out and the media has been calling. It's been crazy."

"Why didn't you say something?" He and Dana had been in contact by satellite phone at least four or five times over the past three weeks. And he'd been a simple email away for the past two days.

"I decided to wait until you got home. I haven't said anything to Ryan and Rogan either, although considering how the news is spreading, they'll probably both hear about it before I can tell them in person."

"Mum," Mal said. "She knows?"

Dana nodded. "She's a little upset over all the attention. They've been calling and wanting to talk to her, but so far she's refused to comment. She's coming to stay with me for the weekend."

The media attention made sense. Maxwell Quinn had been one of the most renowned climbers of his generation and, in the early '90s, only one of a handful of men who had completed the Seven Summits in less than a year. Max's partner, Roger Innis, had used the media coverage after Max's death to his advantage, claiming that Max had died trying to rescue a client. With all the publicity, Outbound Adventure had suddenly become a high-profile guiding company.

But because of a badly written business agreement, Lydie Quinn had been left with virtually nothing. All the business assets went to Innis, and though Max was supposed to have had a life insurance policy through the company, Innis had stopped paying the premiums a few months before the Everest expedition. So Lydie had been forced to sell their little house in Rotorua and move the family back to Auckland, where they'd lived with Mal's grandparents.

Though they'd moved away from their childhood home, Max Quinn's sons couldn't forget his legacy. So they'd started their own adventure guiding business, the name a nod to their father—Maximum Adrenaline. In deference to their mother, they refused to return to Everest, but with only two eight-thousand-foot expeditions on their trip list, it had been hard to compete with Innis's company.

The family's relationship with Roger Innis became almost hostile when they became competitors, with Outbound Adventure doing all it could to win the battle for clients and reputation.

But Innis took chances, sometimes putting his clients at risk in order to get them to the top of a mountain. The Quinns were known to err on the side of caution, and for climbers who paid dearly to get to the summit, this was not always a popular choice. Nor was it flashy enough to get them the media coverage they needed to expand their business.

But they were getting it now, weren't they?

Mal sat down on the front steps and ran his fingers through his hair. "I'm not sure what to say."

"Well, you'd better come up with something. We're going to have to make a statement to the media at some point. I didn't think it was my place, and Mum just refuses to talk about it."

"All right. The next person who calls, have them ring my mobile and I'll make a statement."

"There's something else," she murmured.

"Please tell me the business is bankrupt or my house has burned to the ground. I'd be much more equipped to cope."

"Innis announced that he's going to mount an expedition to recover Dad's effects."

Mal felt as if he'd been punched in the stomach, his breath leaving him. "What the hell? Where does he get off? It's his fault Dad is dead. Does he think he can make up for that by rescuing him now? He should have done his job twenty years ago."

There had been whispers all those years ago, comments from other climbers about Innis's reckless disregard for his partner's safety. They'd said he'd made decisions that had directly contributed to Max Quinn's death. But those had only been rumors; no one knew the real story except for Roger Innis and Mal's father—and neither one of them was talking.

Dana wrapped her arm around Mal's and leaned against him. "It's just talk," she said. "Publicity. You know how he is—he'll use anything to get his business in the news. Just last month he had the cover story in *High Adventure* magazine for his Antarctica expedition."

"The cover?" Mal cursed. "How the hell does he manage that?" Mal had been trying to get a feature in *High Adventure* for years. Mal was convinced the glossy American magazine was key to capturing more American clientele. "I suppose he's hoping for another cover with this harebrained scheme of his. The bludger."

"He can't mount a trip to Everest until at least next spring, and even then, he'd have to get permits and shuffle his clients around. By then all the interest will have died down and—"

"He wants Dad's journal," Mal muttered. "He's well aware Dad kept it in his climbing suit and he's afraid of what might be written there. Innis has worked all these years to rebuild his reputation. He's not going to let it all fall apart now."

The sound of a phone ringing echoed from the office and Dana stood up. "Probably another reporter."

"Do you want me to handle it?" Mal asked.

"No. You're just home. You deserve a chance to relax a bit. I'll tell them what I've been saying for three weeks. No comment. Although that seems to make them even more determined to get a quote." She paused. "You know, maybe we should give an interview. All of us, Mum, too. The publicity couldn't hurt. We could beat Innis at his own game."

"Maybe," he murmured.

"And *High Adventure* magazine has rung three times in the past few days. I told the girl you'd be back tomorrow. Maybe you should talk to her."

A feature article about their father and the Quinn family business might finally bring them out of the shadow of Roger Innis. Especially if they mounted their own expedition. Maybe it was time they learned the truth about that week on Everest.

But did he really want to know? It wouldn't change anything. His father would still be dead and he'd force his mother to relive the tragedy all over again. And he'd promised her that he and his brothers would never climb Everest. There were so many reasons not to go.

Yet Mal couldn't help but wonder if learning the truth—his father's truth—might not put to rest some of the pain he and his family had suffered. Could the answers be found in his father's journal? Had he written his farewells there before he died on the mountain? There were so many unanswered questions.

"I'm going to go see Mum," Mal said, pushing to his feet. "And then I'm going home to grab a shower and a drink, and maybe I'll get myself a haircut."

"What about the woman?" Dana asked with a wry smile.

"That might have to wait," he murmured.

Mal gave Duff a rough pet and the dog trotted beside him to the Range Rover. "You want me to take him?"

"No, I'll keep him."

He waved at his sister, Duffy at her side, as he drove out to the main road. Life had always been pretty uncomplicated for Mal and he liked it that way. But the reality of their business problems was beginning to weigh on him. There was never extra money; he could barely afford to make rent from month to month. When finances were tight, he bought new equipment instead of food and ate expired rations from their expedition stockpile.

He reached into his pocket and grabbed the wad of cash that he had left over from the client tips he and the other guides had divided amongst themselves. He'd take enough for a single night out. The rest would have to go to pay the bills.

"I'd better make it a bloody good night," he muttered. "I've had enough of living like a damn monk."

"HEY, BILLY FINSTER! Set me up with a pint and make it quick. I've got myself a powerful thirst!"

The shout echoed through the empty pub and Amy Engalls looked up from her laptop at the tall, lanky man who strode up to the bar. His hair was shaggy and he wore a well-worn T-shirt and faded jeans. The cap on his head was turned backward and his eyes were hidden by a pair of bright blue sunglasses.

He glanced around and his eyes lingered on her for a long moment. Amy grabbed a quick breath and held it. Was this Malcolm Quinn? He wasn't due back until tomorrow, but she'd studied the photos and it could be him. Word around town was that he and his brothers hung out at Brawley's Pub near his place on the beach. So she'd decided to stake it out. When he turned away, she quickly pulled a file folder from her bag and searched for a reference.

Her breath slowly escaped as she stared down at the handsome face in the photo, then compared it to the profile of the man at the bar.

An instant later, the barkeeper burst through the swinging kitchen door and confirmed her suspicions. "Mal Quinn, you old dog. I was wonderin' when you'd roll back in. Where was it you were?"

"Greenland," Mal said as he slid onto a stool.

The barkeeper drew him a glass of beer and set the pint in front of him. "Bloody hell, what's in Greenland?"

Mal took off his sunglasses and tossed them on the bar. "Lots of ice. And snow and cold."

"Any pretty girls?"

Mal laughed. "Not that I saw. The whole expedition was blokes. Not a woman for miles."

Billy nodded, then slapped his hands on the worn wood surface of the bar. "At that is exactly the reason why you'll never find me out there, trudging up some mountainside or walking across some bloody glacier. I can't do without female companionship. And they can't do without me."

"You can't do without your smokes and Foster's for more than a day," Mal teased. "It's hard yakka out there. Not for a piker like you."

The barkeeper frowned, then patted his stomach. "I could get in shape for it. Give up the ale and the cigs. You could put me with a group of ladies and I'd keep them all entertained."

Amy listened as they exchanged jibes, silently taking in Mal's appearance. How would she describe him in her story? Tall, graceful, fit. He was thin but muscular, broad shouldered and narrow hipped. His dark hair was long and shaggy and streaked by the sun, and his tanned face was shadowed by the stubble of a beard.

He was, by all accounts, one of the most gorgeous men she'd ever seen. The pictures she had didn't come close to conveying the energy that surrounded him. He was powerful and focused, even in casual conversation. Here was a man who lived life to the fullest, a man who wasn't afraid of danger. A man she wanted.

She shifted uneasily, surprised by the depth of her attraction to him. It wasn't just his looks. It was something deeper, more perplexing. Maybe she admired his courage because she had never had much of her own. She'd spent her entire life accepting what was tossed her way and had never really stood up for herself.

Until now, she hoped. She was here to change the course of her life. And she wasn't about to let opportunity slip by, even if it meant approaching an impossibly sexy man and convincing him to do something he wouldn't want to do.

A phone rang and Billy moved to the end of the bar to answer it. Amy continued to observe Mal Quinn from her spot at her table, wondering how she ought to introduce herself. Should she take the initiative now, or wait until tomorrow? What if she didn't get another chance?

She'd worked as a copy editor for *High Adventure* magazine for the past six years, hoping for her big break into feature writing. But most of the feature writers were adventurers themselves, out in the world, doing daring deeds and living to tell their tales. She was just an ordinary girl who could write a really good story. An ordinary girl who just happened to be the publisher's daughter.

Amy had never wanted to write for an adventure magazine. In truth, she would have been happy working at any one of the numerous women's publications that her father owned. But with her father's twisted sense of purpose, he'd put an impossible goal in front of her and challenged her to meet it, all the while assuming she'd fail. That was the way it had always been with Richard Engalls. He wanted his children to prove they were worthy of his valuable attention. Her brother had been a model student and was an adventurer himself.

But Amy didn't seem to possess the Engalls backbone. She was her mother's daughter, still scarred by her parents' divorce when she was thirteen, still hoping that her father might notice her and approve.

Which was why she was here. Amy knew a good story when she read one. And just because she'd never been on a big adventure didn't mean she couldn't write an adventure story, did it? For the first time in her life, she'd show her father that she had what it took to succeed in publishing. She'd cashed in her savings and wagered it on one bet—that she could land a feature with the Quinn brothers. She'd follow their journey, documenting the story of the three Quinn brothers in regular articles. It had everything her editor looked for in a feature—conflict, emotion, a high-profile location and adventurers with personality.

Her editor had scoffed at the notion that Amy could get an exclusive *and* convince her father to fund the expedition. But beneath his bluster, she could tell the editor had found her idea intriguing, and she didn't doubt that he'd go to her father at the first available opportunity and ask for the story himself. But Amy was one step ahead of both of them. She took her two weeks of vacation and, after checking Mal Quinn's online itinerary, bought a plane ticket from New York to Auckland.

Gathering her courage, she pushed her chair back and walked to the bar. She'd order something to eat and maybe strike up a conversation with Mal. She'd almost reached a spot beside him when his mobile rang. He fished it out of his pocket and then slid off the stool and walked to the front door, stepping out into the afternoon sunshine.

Amy groaned inwardly. She was no good at this. Give her a manuscript and she could make it pulse with excitement. She was better with words than people, and she'd never been comfortable talking to strangers. And now, because of her dithering, she'd lost her chance. Mal Quinn had walked out the door. What if he didn't come back? Even worse, what if he did?

Talking to a handsome, sexy man wasn't exactly her forte. Her palms sweated and her heart pounded in her chest and every rational thought just slipped out of her head. It was a wonder she'd managed to have relationships at all. She had, though they were never anything she wanted to make permanent.

When Billy the barkeeper returned from his phone call, Amy slid onto a stool.

"What can I get you, darlin'?" he asked. "Another diet cola?"

"I—I thought I'd have something to eat. Do you have any specials today?"

"Bangers and mash, mussels in cream sauce and a crispy salmon patty. The soup is a crab chowder. The kitchen opens for supper in another half hour. I can probably scratch up a sammie for you or some potato fries if you can't wait."

"I'll just have a bag of crisps," Amy said. "And a beer. Whatever you have on tap."

She needed the drink. Diet cola wasn't going to give her any courage at all. It only made her jittery. She drew a deep breath, then heard the door open behind her. Afraid to look, Amy tried to appear nonchalant.

Billy brought her the beer and crisps. "That'll be six dollars."

"I'll get it."

She froze as she heard his voice behind her. Slowly, Amy turned, and her gaze met his. Oh, hell, he was even more handsome close up. He had that rugged, outdoorsy thing going on. The kind of man that just oozed masculinity. He probably smelled like fresh air and soap and woodsmoke.

Amy wanted to speak, but she couldn't seem to catch her breath. She gulped some air and felt the blood rush to her head as he came closer. Oh, he did smell good. But like cologne, subtle and musky.

Was she supposed to accept his gesture? Was that why he was regarding her so strangely? "I—I have money," Amy finally managed to say.

"So do I," he said with a crooked smile. "I'm just back from a month away and I've got tips burning a hole in my pocket. I reckoned I'd buy the house a drink."

"There's only two of us here," she said.

He leaned closer. "I know. The perfect plan, don't you think?"

"Thank you," she murmured, grabbing her beer and crisps. "And—and welcome home."

She hurried back to her table, needing just a moment to regroup. All right, he was handsome and very charming. And that smile was enough to melt any woman's resistance. But that didn't mean she couldn't act like a professional.

Amy fixed her attention on her computer screen, afraid to risk another glance. The problem was, she really wasn't a professional journalist. She knew exactly what made for a perfect story, she could even write a perfect story. She'd just never gone out and *found* a story. There were probably all sorts of tricks that journalists used to get their subject to confess all their deepest secrets. She just had no idea what those tricks were. She'd been more worried about beating her father and her editor to the story than to research journalistic practices.

Should she introduce herself right off the bat or should she get friendly with him first and ease her way into an interview? Maybe she could just get him to talk about his work or his family and he wouldn't even realize she was interviewing him. Was that ethical? Probably not, but it might be the only way she could get what she needed.

"So what are you staring at? You seem awfully intent on that screen. Let me guess. Porn?"

Amy froze, then slowly looked up. "No, not porn. It's my work computer. I can't watch porn on my work computer. That would be against the rules."

"Do you always follow the rules, then?"

"I—I try to," Amy murmured. Mal pulled out the chair across from her, turned it around and straddled the seat. He rested his arm across the back and took a slow sip of his beer. "Go ahead. Carry on. I don't want to interrupt your work."

Amy's heart slammed in her chest as she refocused on the screen in front of her. Here he was, ready to talk. Now she just had to keep up her end of the conversation. "Thank you for the drink—and the crisps." She glanced up to find him grinning at her. "What?"

"Nothing," Malcolm replied. "I'm just enjoying the view."

She scanned the room. "I—I don't understand."

Then she realized he was talking about her. Amy's face flushed with embarrassment.

"I haven't seen a beautiful woman in a month, so I'm just going to sit here and stare at you, if you don't mind. I'll try not to bother you."

Pretty? Did he really think she was pretty? She'd never really applied that term to herself. She wasn't unattractive, just…ordinary.

"You must have been gone longer than a month if you think I'm pretty," she murmured, unable to keep herself from returning the smile.

"Aw, now, don't say that. You're lovely."

She glanced around the pub. "I don't have much competition," she countered.

"Well, I happen to be a very good judge of beauty. I've seen some of the most beautiful places in the world. So trust me on this."

"Thank you," Amy said. "For the crisps and the compliment."

"I'm Mal Quinn, by the way," he said, holding out his hand.

"Nice to meet you," Amy said.

A long silence fell between them as she tried to decide what to do. In the end, she didn't have a choice, the introduction just came out. "I'm Amy Engalls. I'm a reporter from *High Adventure* magazine and I've come here to interview you."

She quickly grabbed his hand and shook it, then held on tight, hoping that he wouldn't get up and walk out the door.

He studied her silently, as if he needed time to form a response. "Well, I certainly didn't expect that." Mal slowly got to his feet. "I suppose you want a quote. I'll make it quick and painless. No comment."

He pulled out of her grasp and headed toward the door. Amy hurried after him. "Wait. I'm sorry. Let me explain."

"No explanation necessary," he muttered. "Billy, it was nice seeing you again."

The barkeeper watched them, confused. "You goin' already, Mal?"

"Yeah. The place is a little quiet for my tastes right now. I'll be back later." He set his glass on the bar and walked out.

Amy looked at Billy and groaned. "I'm sorry," she called.

"What the hell did you say to him?" Billy asked.

"No comment." She hurried over to her table and gathered her things, hoping she could catch up to him. A real reporter wouldn't give up her story without a fight, and neither would Amy.

THE MOMENT MAL got outside the pub, he let out a long string of profanities. He'd realized he'd have to deal with this sooner or later, but he hadn't expected it this soon. What the hell was a reporter doing here, in his hometown? The story must be much bigger than he'd ever assumed.

And how the hell was he supposed to react? He and his family had dealt with the loss for nearly twenty years now, and yet the pain hadn't dulled at all. There were still the "what ifs," all the possible scenarios that could have unfolded that day on the mountain that could have resulted in a different outcome. Those were the worst.

What might it have been like to grow up with a father? It wasn't as if his childhood had been bad. There'd just been a huge, gaping hole in his family that Max Quinn should have filled. How was he supposed to explain these things to a total stranger? This wasn't about some frozen body on Mount Everest. This was about his father.

"Mr. Quinn!"

He spun around to find the reporter running toward him. In the next instant, she stumbled over a crack in the pavement and before he could reach to help her, she went down, face-first. "Oh, hell," Mal muttered, racing to her side.

By the time he got to her, she had managed to sit up, but both her knees were scraped and bleeding and her computer was in pieces around her. "Oh, no," she said, picking up the shattered bits of plastic.

"Are you all right? Did you hit your head?"

She reached up and touched her forehead. "No, I don't think so."

"Anything broken? Does it hurt anywhere?"

"Just my pride," she said, wincing.

He met her eyes and his anger softened. She was only trying to do her job. Maybe he shouldn't have been so rude. "Can you stand?"

She nodded her head. He took her hand and helped her to her feet. "Thank you."

"What's your name again?"

"Amy Engalls."

"Amy Engalls from *High Adventure,*" Mal said. "Any relation to Richard Engalls, the publisher?"

"He's my father," she said.

"And that would make David Engalls your brother?"

"Yes," she said.

Richard Engalls had built his media empire, in part, to fund his love of adventure. He'd circumnavigated the globe in a balloon, had attempted to row across the Atlantic, and had climbed all Seven Summits. He'd also funded a number of expeditions and was the go-to investor in adventure expeditions after the National Geographic Society. Mal had also met David Engalls, the younger version of his father, who was very good at spending millions of Daddy's money on his own exotic adventures. Mal's opinion of David was that he was a horse's arse—but a very wealthy horse's arse. Mal had never known there was a daughter involved in the business, as well.

He reached down to brush the dust off her skirt, moving to a spot on her backside before he realized what he was doing. She had a very nice bum, as bums went. In fact, there wasn't much about Amy Engalls that he found unattractive—beyond her profession. "Come on. Let's get those scrapes fixed. I live just down the road. I've got antiseptic and bandages."

"I'll be fine," she said.

"If I were you, Amy Engalls, I'd accept my offer. And while I'm bandaging your knees, you can try to get a comment out of me."

This brought a smile to her pretty face. "All right."

He picked up the pieces of her computer and then led her to the Range Rover. She groaned in pain as he helped her climb up into the passenger seat. Mal jogged around to his side and hopped in, then started the car.

As they headed out of town, he glanced over at her.

She was pretty. Not overblown gorgeous, but cute in a clean, girl-next-door way. Her pale hair fell in waves around her face, framing eyes that were an odd mix of green and blue. Although none of her features were particularly striking, when put together, they made a face that he found very pleasant to look at.

As for her body, she was slender, but there were curves in the right places. Coming from a climbing family, he expected her to be lean and wiry, the kind of woman who could hold her own on a mountainside. But instead, she seemed soft and feminine despite clothes that did nothing to enhance her figure.

"So tell me about yourself, Amy Engalls. Do you share your family's love of adventure?"

"Oh, yes," she said.

"What was the last mountain you stumbled up?"

She laughed softly. "Very funny. I'm not always so clumsy. I studied ballet. I'm just not used to…running."

"I can see that. That was quite a fall you took."

"I wasn't actually running, I was chasing. You," she said.

"Oh, and now you're blaming me?"

"No, I just wanted to explain."

"That you studied ballet?"

"No, why I came here to interview you."

"You have me alone right now. It's as good a moment as any. Have at it."

She didn't say anything for a long time and Mal waited, wondering what her first question might be. "I'm not sure I can do this," she finally said.

"Do what?"

"Pry into your personal life," she said.

"You're not a top-notch chaser, and if you won't pry, you won't get very far as a reporter, either."

She straightened in her seat. "All right. Tell me how you felt when you heard the news that they'd found your father."

"My father's body," he corrected. Mal could explain exactly how he'd felt. He just wasn't sure he wanted to start blathering on about it. From the time of his father's death, he and his family had always maintained a stiff upper lip. Max Quinn had died doing what he loved, that was what they'd always said. And no one ever knew when he'd go. He could be hit by a bus tomorrow.

And yet, what had that answer ever gotten them?

Mal glanced over at her and sighed softly. "The answer would be…gobsmacked."

"It must have brought back a lot of memories."

"He's never been far from my mind," Mal admitted.

In truth, his father's memory had loomed large in Mal's life. Max Quinn was a legend, a man everyone had assumed was invincible. Hell, he was the bloody Titanic of mountain climbing, the guy who could conquer any peak and do it with a smile.

And the climbing community had expected Mal to take after his father, to court risk, to laugh at danger. But even though Mal wanted to do his father proud, he knew what another loss would do to his family. Yes, he was carrying on his father's legacy. But would Max Quinn have been proud?

"It's been a long time," she said.

"I was ten when he died. My siblings don't remember him as well as I do."

"He was just six years older than you are now when he died."

"Thirty-six," Mal murmured. Jesus, she was right. His father had already accomplished so much by that age. He'd founded a successful business and had been up and down Everest five times. And what did Mal have to show for his life? A struggling business? A dwindling clientele? He didn't need to conquer Everest to carry on his father's legacy. He just needed to run a successful guiding business. At least that was what he'd always told himself.

As they pulled up to Mal's small "bach" on the beach, he thought of his father, with so much of his life in front of him, with a wife and family back in New Zealand. Had he been flooded with regret in his last moments? Or had he been satisfied that he'd died doing something he loved?

Mal shut off the Range Rover, then rested his hands on the wheel. "Some people said that he was a selfish man. That he should have given up climbing the moment he got married and had children. What do you think?" he asked.

"I think that some people are driven to make something out of their lives. And others are content with what they're given along the way."

"And what kind of man am I?" he asked.

"I can't say," Amy said. "We've only just met." She paused, then shook her head. "That was a rhetorical question, wasn't it?"

"Maybe not," Mal said, opening the car door. "If you come up with an answer, let me know."

He helped Amy out of the car, grabbing the pieces

of her computer as she slid down to the ground. They walked slowly up to the cottage and he pointed to a wooden rocker on the wide porch. "Sit. I'll be right back."

He pulled open the screen door and stepped inside. Reporters were all alike, only interested in getting the story they wanted and never worrying about the people involved. Even now, he remembered those days after his father's death, how they'd been hounded by the media hoping to get photos of the grieving mother and her children. Lydie Quinn had been so upset, she'd refused to let her children leave the house, depending upon friends to bring them what they needed. So Mal knew he shouldn't trust her.

Yet even though she was a reporter, Mal couldn't deny that he found her attractive. And she didn't seem like the kind of cutthroat opportunist that most journalists were. She was...sweet. And he found the "damsel in distress" thing sexy as hell.

"Don't fool yourself, Mal," he muttered as he rummaged through a tin of first-aid supplies.

When he returned to Amy, she was bent over, examining her injuries more closely. "It's not so bad," she said.

He squatted down in front of her, then sprayed antiseptic onto both knees. She winced and Mal leaned in and blew on her wounds, hoping to take away the sting. "Better?"

"Mmm," she said, nodding.

He carefully bandaged the scrapes, then slowly ran his hand from knee to ankle. She had beautiful legs, slender yet shapely. He couldn't seem to help himself and he ran his hand up her calf, enjoying the feel of her flesh beneath his fingers.

When he heard her suck in a sharp breath, Mal risked a look up and found her staring at him, wide-eyed. "It should be good now," he murmured. He sat back on his heels. "I could use a drink. Would you like one?"

"Sure," she said. "Water would be fine. Or a diet cola."

"I was thinking about something a bit stronger. Whiskey, perhaps."

"Oh, whiskey would be fine," she said.

Mal straightened, his gaze still locked on hers. He ought to just kiss her now and be done with it. He'd never been the kind of guy to hide his desires. When he wanted a woman, he made it clear from the start. And what was there to stop them? They were two consenting adults. At least, he was consenting.

Mal cursed inwardly. Was he reading her wrong? Was she playing him just to get her story? He could see she was attracted…tempted. But maybe she was trying to be "professional." "I'm going to go get those drinks," he said.

2

AMY PUSHED TO her feet and walked to the rail of the porch, staring out at the water. The sun was dropping closer to the horizon and the sunset colors painted the sky in a blaze of orange and pink.

He lived in paradise, she mused. Though the cottage, or bach as he called it, was small, the location couldn't be beat. But then, Mal probably took stunning scenery for granted.

Her thoughts returned to his comment at the bar, the sideways compliment he'd given her. Mal Quinn had said she was pretty. What did that mean? She knew how it felt. An odd anticipation had settled over her, as if she was waiting for something she wasn't sure she wanted.

It wasn't difficult to read his intentions. He'd been on a glacier for the past month with a bunch of guys. He'd rubbed her calf and now he was getting them both a drink.

But if Amy knew only one thing about being a reporter, it was that you didn't sleep with the subject of your story. She had to maintain professional objectivity, and she couldn't do that if she was constantly undressing Mal Quinn in her mind.

She closed her eyes and drew a deep breath, the images floating through her head. There had been a number of men in her life, but they'd all been rather ordinary—an accountant, a lawyer and the owner of a bookstore. Not the kind of guys who hung off the sides of mountains for a living. They didn't even venture outside when it was raining.

Mal Quinn was a passionate man. And someone who lived his life on the edge would certainly bring that same intensity to the bedroom. A shiver skittered down her spine at the idea of the two of them together. There was a bed inside his cottage, probably just ten or fifteen short steps away.

The door opened and Mal stepped out onto the porch, a bottle and two tumblers in his hands. He held a glass out to her and then poured a small measure of whiskey into it. After he poured himself a drink, he sat down in the chair next to hers.

They sat silently for a long time, staring out at the sunset. Amy was afraid to talk, sensing that he was still considering her offer to be featured in the magazine. Or was he considering something else? Maybe he was undressing her in his head.

Amy winced inwardly. She didn't spend a lot of time working out or watching her diet. He was probably used to women who could free-climb a rock wall or trek to the South Pole. There were days when she could barely make it from the subway to her office without complete exhaustion.

"This is a beautiful country," she said. "Everything is so…wild. Untamed. Unspoiled—"

"I'm not going to do your story," Mal said. "I can't."

"Someone is going to write about this," she said. "With me, you could get your story out there the way you *want* it to be told."

Mal shook his head. "It took my mum a year to make it through the day without crying. I'm not going to make her relive that time. You can write what you want to write, but without me or my brothers."

"Without you, there's no story," Amy murmured.

"You're not going to write anything?"

Amy shook her head. "I know good stories, and that wouldn't be a good story. I wanted to write about your father and the aftereffects of the tragedy that took his life." She shrugged. "I understand that wouldn't be easy for you."

She didn't want to give up, but Amy saw the pain in his expression. The emotions were still raw, the wounds unhealed even after twenty years. She was sure in her heart she could tell their story the right way, putting aside the sensational and focusing on the human element. But if he wasn't going to participate, what was the point?

Amy pushed to her feet. "I should probably go. I can't afford to miss any more work."

"Isn't this your work?"

She didn't want to admit the truth to him, but then again, what difference did it make now? "I was hoping if I got this story, I could convince my father to mount an expedition to Everest for you and your brothers."

He gasped, then looked away. Gulping down the last

of his whiskey, Mal sat silently for a long moment. Amy waited, wondering if the revelation might change his mind. "I thought we'd do a series of articles. Profiles on all three of you, then we'd follow the preparations for the expedition. And then cover the expedition itself. I wanted to put a historical perspective on the story and show the way climbing Everest has changed in the past twenty years."

"You have a lot of grand plans," he said.

"I do," Amy admitted.

Was he really considering her offer? Would the expedition change his mind? Amy knew she ought to tell him the truth, that an Everest trip wasn't actually a firm part of the deal, but if she wanted this story, then she had to do everything in her power to make it happen. That was what a real journalist did.

"I'm still not going to do the story," he said.

Frustration welled up inside her. So he'd decided to string her along and get her drunk. "Then I think I'll go back to my hotel." She walked down the porch steps, then realized that she didn't have her car. And she wasn't really sure how to get back to her hotel.

"Come on," Mal said. "At least let me buy you dinner for your trouble. You came all the way to New Zealand."

"You already bought me crisps and a beer. I'm good."

Mal jogged down the steps and grabbed her hand. The physical contact sent a tremor through her body. When he leaned closer, she forgot to breathe. She realized she should put some distance between them. And yet she couldn't seem to make herself move.

She wanted him to kiss her, to come away with that one singular experience. She'd consider her trip a mild success if she left with that memory. After all, this whole trip had been about expanding her horizons, about reaching for new goals.

"Can I take you out?" he asked. "I promise, I'll show you a good time."

She couldn't help but smile. If he knew the kind of fun that she had in mind, he might not be so anxious to keep her around. Or maybe he would....

Glancing down at their hands, her fingers still caught up in his, Amy realized what she had to do. If she couldn't have the story, then she'd satisfy herself with the man. Or at least a night out with him. Suddenly, the word *adventure* took on a whole new meaning.

"All right," she said. "I am hungry."

Mal gave her hand a squeeze, then pulled her along to the Range Rover. "A friend of mine has a burger place over on Bow Street. Do you like burgers? Of course you do, you're American. You're going to love this place."

He opened the door and helped her into the truck. Amy watched as he jogged around to the driver's side. He moved with such ease, as if he was in absolute control of every muscle in his body. What would it feel like to have that body beside her in bed? To be able to touch him at will?

As he slid in behind the wheel, she pushed the thought out of her head. She'd blown all of this entirely out of proportion. He'd touched her calf; he'd squeezed her hand. That didn't mean he wanted to carry her into his bed and ravish her. It was Mal Quinn's business to be charming and accommodating. They would have a fun meal, that was all.

She searched her mind for a topic of conversation.

Now that he'd refused the article, she didn't want to probe his past too deeply. She took a different tack. "Do you surf?"

"Yes," he said. "After my father died, we moved up from the south island. My mum's parents lived here and we lived with them at first. They ran a little restaurant."

"Does your whole family still live here?"

"My grandparents have a place closer to Auckland now. The bach was theirs. They used to rent rooms out to visiting surfers. Now my brothers live there with me, although we're rarely there together. And my younger sister also lives in town with a few friends. She used to live with us, but that didn't really work out once she started bringing men home."

"Your father was Australian. Do you ever see that side of the family?"

He glanced over at her. "You've done your research."

She smiled. "I wanted to be prepared."

"He was an only child and his mother passed away when he was thirteen. He never knew his father. He lived with foster families for a couple of years, then ran away when he was sixteen. He just wandered from adventure to adventure after that, working when he had to. He ended up in New Zealand, where he met Roger Innis, and the rest is history."

Amy wanted paper and a pen to take notes, but since she'd managed to gain his trust, she had to keep it. "That adds a whole new context to his life," she said. "I've always wondered what drives a man to risk his life for...thrills."

"I couldn't tell you."

"You don't feel that thrill?"

He shook his head. "Not the kind of thrill that makes me want to risk my life. Don't get me wrong, I love what I do. I love seeing new and beautiful places, and I love showing those places to other people. But it's not about me, it's about the clients. With my father, I think it was about him. Even when he had clients with him."

They pulled up in front of the restaurant and Mal parked the car and turned off the ignition. He stared out the windshield, a perplexed expression on his face. He laughed softly. "You know, I never really made the connection before, between his childhood and his need to tempt the fates."

"I can understand his urge," she said. "Maybe, after all that had happened to him as a kid, he was a little numb. Risking his life made him feel alive."

He twisted in his seat, facing her. "But why have a family? Why put them at risk, too?"

"That's easy," Amy said. "Love. He lost his mother when he was young. I suppose he always wanted a family again, and when he met your mother, that happened. It just didn't heal all the wounds." She shook her head. "I'm not a psychologist, so this is all speculative. I guess we'll never really know."

"My father kept journals. My mother said she burned them, but I believe she still has them. They might provide more insight."

"Maybe you should ask her if you can read them," Amy said. "It might give you the peace you need."

He considered her suggestion for a long moment. And then, without any warning, he reached out and pulled her toward him. His lips met hers and she realized that he was kissing her.

His tongue gently probed and she eagerly joined in. He was everything she'd imagined he would be—warm and passionate and powerful. He caressed her face with his hands as he deepened his assault and Amy sighed, the sound swallowed by the kiss.

When he finally drew back, she was light-headed and breathless. She wanted to kiss him again and keep kissing him until…until they found something more exciting to do. She leaned into him and he immediately took the cue and captured her mouth in another deep, delicious encounter.

This time, when he drew back, she held fast to the front of his shirt. They couldn't go on until she understood exactly where she stood with him. "What are the chances you're going to do this story with me?" she asked. "Just give me the odds."

"As much as you've made an enticing pitch, I just can't," Mal said.

"Then I suppose there's nothing to stop you from kissing me again."

He grinned. "There was nothing stopping me before," Mal replied.

"All right, then, carry on," she said.

With a low growl, he shook his head. "I think maybe we should go inside and have dinner."

Amy drew a deep breath. "Right. Let's have dinner."

A meal would give her an opportunity to regroup and figure out what the hell she was doing. If the story was a no-go, then she was free to pursue other avenues with Mal Quinn. Sexual avenues…and boulevards…and expressways. She'd come to New Zealand to make a major change in her life. Maybe she should start with herself.

MAL HAD BEGUN the evening searching for a warm body to take to bed. To his surprise, he'd found a funny, smart and sexy woman. Too bad she was a journalist.

He watched in amusement as she tackled the huge hamburger, digging into her dinner with enthusiasm.

"It's good, right?" he asked.

"Really good," she said.

"New Zealand beef. It's the best."

"I think all the cheese and truffle oil might have something to do with it, too," she said, closely examining the burger.

They sat on the wide front porch of the restaurant, which overlooked the street. Raglan was a typical surf haven, filled with funky shops and casual restaurants. The laid-back atmosphere was exactly what he needed when he came home from an expedition, these surroundings providing the perfect atmosphere to decompress.

Though he'd been to many breathtaking spots in the world, home was always the most beautiful to him. He'd grown up here, learned to surf here and made plans for his first solo adventure in the cozy bach on the beach.

"I've never seen a woman eat like that," he said.

"Then you haven't been hanging around real women," Amy countered. "Not all of us eat like rabbits."

"I reckon not," he said. He respected that about Amy. She didn't try to turn herself into someone she assumed he wanted. She was true and genuine. "So tell me about your travels. I've read about your father and your brother. What about you?"

She gazed across the table at him, an odd expression on her face. "I'd much rather hear about your trip to Greenland. That sounds interesting."

"It was," he said. "At the rate the glaciers are melting, there will come a day when that trip isn't possible. I'm glad I'm able to give people the experience before it's too late."

"What's your favorite trip?" she asked.

"Every trip has something special," he said. "It's not the scenery, it's more the feeling. I'll be standing in some marketplace in Nepal or talking to some Argentinian farmer and I'll say to myself, what the bloody hell am I doing here? I can't believe I live this life."

"Have you ever thought of settling down and staying in one place?"

Mal shook his head. "Never. I make my living as a guide and even though I'm very careful, there are still dangers. I'd never put someone through what my mother went through."

"Do you think she regrets marrying your father?"

"No. They loved each other. And she understood what she was getting into when they got married. But I do think it might have been easier if they hadn't had children."

"How can you say that? You and your siblings are a part of him that lives on."

It was so odd to talk about these matters, especially with a virtual stranger. And yet discussing his father with Amy had already given him new insights. Until now, he'd been pretty rigid in his opinions, but he was starting to realize that it was not always black-and-white.

The subject turned to his business and Amy was

curious about the expeditions his company offered. Though she knew a great deal about the locations, Mal got the impression that she hadn't done a lot of adventuring herself. Or maybe she was just trying to keep him talking. Either way, he didn't mind. She had a way of making him feel completely comfortable. There was no question she might ask that he wouldn't answer.

Which was dangerous. She was a reporter after all. And he couldn't be completely certain about her motives. Though this flirtation was fun, Mal wasn't sure he was willing to take it to the next level.

But why not? If she was willing, why not enjoy a night of passion before she went home? Having sex with her certainly wasn't going to change his mind. And he was positive they'd have a great time indulging in the desire that was growing more intense with every minute that passed.

He reached out and snagged her hand, hooking his little finger around hers. "Why don't we walk off this meal? We can go get your car and you can follow me back to the house. I'll show you my beach."

The waitress brought the bill and though Amy insisted on paying, Mal couldn't agree. He wanted this to be a real date, not just two people sharing a casual meal. He'd follow dinner with a romantic stroll on the beach and that would lead to more kissing and touching. And maybe, after all that, she'd end up in his bed.

They walked down the front steps and Mal linked his fingers through hers. He didn't want to let any opportunity slip by, but Amy needed to know that his intentions were purely carnal. That way, she'd make the choice.

They got in the Range Rover and he pulled it around

and headed toward the pub where they'd met earlier that afternoon. She seemed oddly silent and he risked a glance over at her, wondering if she was reconsidering her choices.

"What's going on in that head of yours?" Mal asked.

"You mentioned your father's journals. Have you ever thought of writing your own book about him?"

Her reply caught him by surprise. Unlike him, she clearly wasn't thinking about sex. She was thinking about business. "I can't write."

"Everyone can write," Amy said. "You'd just need a good editor to help you put things in order."

"Do I know any good editors?"

She sent him a haughty smile.

"Are you volunteering?"

"It's just an idea. But it might be good for you. You'd get to know your father again, only this time with an adult perspective."

"Why is it that everything you say makes perfect sense to me?"

"That's funny, most things I say don't make sense to *me*."

He'd never considered an autobiography, a project that he and his family could control. Maybe it wasn't a bad idea....

They found her car where she'd left it earlier that day. "Just follow me," he said. "It's not far."

She jumped out of the Range Rover and turned to him. "Maybe I should go back to the hotel."

He shook his head. "No. I don't want this night to end quite yet. Take a walk with me. It's just a walk."

"All right."

He watched as she got into her rental car, a sense of anticipation growing inside him. He had every intention of kissing her again. And if that led to something more, he wasn't going to worry about the future. He didn't need just any woman right now, he needed Amy Engalls. She was the only woman who could satisfy him.

But though she appeared to be quite confident and self-assured, there was an underlying vulnerability to her. He saw it in the way she deftly changed the subject when he tried to get her to talk about herself. At first, he'd assumed it was just a reporter's method of always turning the question back on the subject. But over the course of dinner, he'd begun to believe that she figured her life might seem uninteresting to him.

In truth, he wanted to learn everything about her. What did she do on a normal Saturday night? Where did she live? What kind of music did she enjoy? They were all such insignificant questions, but he was curious.

They reached the cottage and he pulled the Range Rover to a stop in the sandy drive, then jumped out and jogged to her car. Mal opened the door and held out his hand, helping her out. "Do you have a cardie or a jacket? It's probably going to be a bit chilly."

"I don't," she said.

"I'll grab you something," he said. "Wait here."

He ran into the house and pulled a fleece jacket from the hook near the door, then grabbed a second for himself. When he returned, she was standing at the bottom of the steps. Mal held out the jacket and she slipped her arms into the sleeves. Then he spun her around and zipped the front.

"Cozy," she said, rubbing her arms.

He glanced down at her bare legs. "Do you want to put on some pants?"

"I'll be fine," she said.

A breeze had come up and it whipped her honey-blond hair around her face. He reached out and tucked a strand behind her ear. "Let's go, then," he said.

Mal held out his hand and she placed her fingers in his. They walked down a sandy path to the beach. The sun had set a few hours before and the stars had come out, pinpricks of light scattered across the inky black sky.

Waves rolled against the shore and they strolled to the edge of the water. She kicked off her shoe and dipped her toe in. "It's cold."

"It never warms up enough to surf without a wetsuit. Not like California or Hawaii."

She kicked off her other shoe and waded in, reaching down to run her fingers through the water. She didn't see the wave rolling in behind her, but Mal did. He figured the water was shallow enough that she could maintain her balance, but the minute the wave hit her calves, her feet got swept out from under her and she fell into the water. She screamed as the wave surrounded her.

Cursing softly, Mal reached her in a few short strides and pulled her upright. Amy clutched his jacket, her hair stuck to her face in damp strands, her breath coming in deep gasps.

And then suddenly, she started laughing, a boisterous giggle that came from deep inside of her. "What is wrong with me?" she shouted. "Why can't I stay on my feet?"

Mal reached down and scooped her up, then carried

her out of the water. "I'm not sure. Maybe you're better off your feet."

She shivered, crossing her arms over her breasts.

"I think we'd better go find you some dry clothes."

"Well, at least I can say I've been swimming in the Indian Ocean. That's a first," she said, wrapping her arms around his neck.

"It's actually the Tasman Sea."

"Even better," Amy said. She brushed the wet hair out of her eyes. "Oh, my shoes!"

"Don't worry, I'll come out in the morning and find them. They'll be washed up on the sand."

"I'm going to need shoes."

"Not tonight," he said. "I don't think you should do any more walking. You might end up in the hospital."

WHEN THEY REACHED the warmth of his cottage, Mal set her down on her feet and quickly stripped off the sodden jacket. The dress she wore beneath clung to her skin, made almost transparent by the damp. Amy plucked at the fabric with her fingers. By now she was cold to the bone and shivering. But the trembles coursing through her body had less to do with the cold and more to do with the way he was looking at her—as if he might devour her at any moment.

"Why don't you jump in the shower and warm up. I'll get you something to wear. The bathroom is just down that hall," he said.

Amy nodded and turned in that direction. But at the last moment, he caught her hand and pulled her into his arms. His mouth came down on hers, only this time, it felt like he was sending her a message: things were about to get much more intimate. If she wanted to leave, she ought to do it now.

Amy didn't need to think twice. She was sure of what she wanted. And to that end, she reached down and began to unbutton her dress. Mal stepped back, his hands resting on her shoulders, his gaze fixed on her fingers.

When she reached the end of the buttons, she glanced up at him, hoping he'd take the next step. To her relief, he did, reaching out and brushing the damp fabric from her shoulder.

His lips found a spot at the base of her neck and Amy tipped her head to the side, enjoying the rush of heat that raced through her body. He caught her fingers in his, raising her hand above her head. Then he reached down, grabbed the hem of her dress and slowly pulled it up and over her arms.

The air hit her damp skin, goose bumps prickling her until she shuddered with the chill. Mal was wet from rescuing her and he kicked off his sodden shoes, then shrugged out of the fleece jacket and T-shirt. Grabbing a faded quilt from the back of the sofa, he wrapped her up in it.

"Better?" he asked.

"Yes," Amy said in a soft voice. "Much."

"Sit," he said.

She did as he asked and Mal knelt down and took her foot in his hand, brushing the sand from between her toes and then gently rubbing until her foot was warm. He did the same for the other foot, and within a few minutes, Amy was no longer shivering.

Until Mal leaned in and pressed a kiss to the curve of her instep.

Amy drew a quick breath and he raised his eyes to meet her gaze. She sighed softly. "That felt good. Do it again." It was the closest she could come to an open invitation. *Go ahead, ravish me,* was what she really wanted to say. But then, that would be very bold, even given her newfound courage.

His lips found the arch of her foot. Though it was an odd way to begin a seduction, to Amy it seemed even more intimate than kissing her mouth. Slowly, his lips traced a path from her foot to the inside of her calf.

When the quilt got in the way, Mal braced his hands on either side of her and brushed a kiss onto the exposed skin of her shoulder. Somewhere in the back of her mind, Amy wondered about the ethics of what she was doing, about the wisdom of sleeping with a man she still wanted to interview. But he'd said himself she wouldn't be able to convince him, and once he touched her, none of it mattered.

Mal's lips found hers again and this time his kiss was a lovely mixture of desire and surrender, soft and sweet, yet filled with unrestrained need. He moved his mouth to her neck, pulling the quilt aside to kiss the spot below her ear.

He cupped her face in his hands and moved back to her mouth. Amy's fingers clutched at his T-shirt, pulling him closer until he was nearly lying on top of her.

It felt wonderful to have the weight of a man's body stretched out over hers. And though she ought to have considered this more carefully, at this point Amy's desire far outweighed her common sense.

"Are you warm enough?" he asked. "Or do you want to take that shower?" He paused. "Or we could crawl under the covers on my bed and I could—"

"Okay," Amy interrupted. "Bed sounds good."

She didn't hesitate and stood up beside the sofa, the quilt still wrapped around her body. Amy could barely catch her breath. It was as if she was tumbling down a mountainside and she couldn't seem to gain a foothold. Things were moving so fast, and she felt as if she'd lost all touch with reality. But now that she'd gained momentum, she didn't want to stop. She couldn't.

There was no use denying the attraction. It had been there from the moment he'd first looked at her. In truth, it had been there from the very first time she'd seen his photograph. He was the kind of guy she could only dream about having—handsome, charming, fearless.

And now she'd been handed the chance to be with him, to experience something she might never find in her life again. Sure, she'd had lovers in the past, but they'd never lived up to her expectations. They'd never made her feel wild and uninhibited. Just once, she wanted to be with a man who could make her heart pound and her body ache.

Just a week ago, she'd been curled up on her sofa in her Brooklyn flat, eating a pint of cherry-chocolate-chip ice cream and watching a string of romantic comedies. That had been her life, waiting for Mr. Right. Well, it was time to stop waiting. She'd found Mr. Right Now here in a bach on the beach in New Zealand.

This wouldn't be about love or even affection. It would about pure, unadulterated passion. This would be the adventure she'd never been brave enough to take, the mountain she'd been too fearful to climb. She wasn't about to pass this opportunity by. If she couldn't leave New Zealand with a story, then she'd leave with a damn good memory.

Mal stopped at the bedroom door and she glanced inside to see a large, comfortable bed covered with a deep down duvet. Mal grabbed her hands and pinned them above her head against the door frame, searching her gaze intently. "Are you sure this is what you want?" he murmured, pressing his hips against hers.

The quilt fell away, leaving Amy dressed only in her damp underwear. She could feel his desire beneath the faded fabric of his jeans. He was already completely aroused. Amy wanted to touch him there, to smooth her fingers over the hard ridge of his erection. She could be bold, too. "Yes," she said, pushing back with her body.

He kissed her again, his lips and tongue demanding a response. She opened beneath the assault and did her best to match his intensity. And when he groaned, Amy knew that *she* was exactly what he wanted. Untangling her fingers from his, she let her hands drop to his shoulders and then his chest.

Gently, she pushed him away, then walked into the bedroom and stood at the end of the bed, facing away from him. With trembling fingers, she reached for the clasp of her bra and unhooked it. A moment later, her panties lay at her feet. She couldn't make her need much more evident. She heard his breath catch as she turned to face him.

A tiny sliver of doubt coursed through her. She'd never been more vulnerable than she was now. But Amy didn't care. For once in her life, she had the courage she'd always wanted. And, as long as he was there, it wasn't going to leave her.

He approached her slowly and Amy's knees began to give way. She wanted to sit down on the end of the bed, but she was afraid to move. As if Mal sensed her distress, he slipped his arm around her waist and drew her against him.

His palms smoothed over her spine, drifting down to her waist and then cupping her backside. The sensation of his touch made every nerve in her body sing with anticipation until she felt as if the tingling would never stop. Gently, he moved her to the bed, then pulled them both down in a tangle of limbs.

As he kissed her again, he began to strip off his clothes. First his T-shirt, then his belt and jeans. She was so distracted by his single-minded assault on her mouth that when he stretched out on top of her, the touch of his skin against hers was a shock.

Amy held her breath, taking it all in. Was this really happening to her? She tried to keep a clear head, knowing that after it was over, she'd want to savor every detail again, but Mal was determined to drive her over the edge with passion.

His lips trailed across her shoulder, then moved lower. She waited for the touch of his tongue on her nipple, but he continued down, halting at the spot between her legs. A moan tore from her throat as his tongue began to tease at her sex.

Amy's body tensed and she felt as if she was about to leap out of her own skin. Every flick, every gentle suck, sent wave after wave of delicious sensation coursing through her. She arched against him, unable to ask for more yet needing him to continue.

He knew exactly what he was doing and he showed no uncertainty. Mal wanted her complete surrender and Amy didn't care what it cost. Her fingers slipped through his thick hair and she coaxed him on as he brought her closer to the edge. Her heart slammed in her chest and her body writhed against his mouth. And suddenly, she was there.

The world exploded in a riot of unbearable sensation, shudders of pleasure racking her body. He continued on until she was desperate to stop, the torment too sweet for her to bear. "Stop," she whispered.

He slowly brought her body down from the peak, the spasms subsiding until she was left boneless and mindless, a victim of his seduction. Mal pressed his lips to the inside of her thigh and she stared down at him.

"That was lovely," he said with a wicked smile.

Amy wasn't sure whether she should laugh or cry. It had been lovely. Better than anything she'd ever experienced in her life. And she wanted to do it again. But she couldn't help the doubts creeping into her head. Had she made a mistake? How was she supposed to live the rest of her life knowing that this was what passion was really about?

After it was all over, she'd have had her adventure. But then what? Was she meant to go home and forget it had ever happened?

No. If she wanted everything, the perfect experience, then it couldn't end here. She could give him as good as she'd got.

Amy pulled him up next to her, stretching out beside

him. Smoothing her hands over his belly, she brushed up against his shaft.

Mal smiled, his eyes still glazed with desire. Wrapping her fingers around him, Amy gently stroked. His response was immediate and he growled softly, nuzzling his face into the curve of her neck.

Her touch was soft and gentle. She wanted to tempt him, but not too far, as there was so much more she needed before he finished. Amy felt powerful, in control. She'd heard stories about climbers, men like Mal who flirted with danger and death. They approached sex in the same way, with a powerful passion that couldn't be denied, as if every moment in bed with a woman might be their last.

She wanted to be the woman he remembered when he was sleeping in his tent on some distant mountainside. She wanted him to imagine her there with him as he pleasured himself on lonely nights.

She pressed her lips to the center of his chest, the soft dusting of hair tickling at the tip of her tongue. As he'd done to her, she moved lower. And when she closed her mouth over the tip of his shaft, Amy realized he was now at her mercy.

He reacted as any man would. But to Amy's surprise, he wasn't a silent participant. He softly urged her on, telling her when it felt good, whispering encouragement. She reveled in the sound of his voice, hearing how she made him feel.

And then suddenly he froze, his body stiffening beneath her touch. Amy knew he was close, fighting back the surge of pleasure that threatened. He held her tight, unwilling to let her continue, and she waited for him to regain control.

When he did, he pulled her up against his body, then reached over to grab a condom from the bedside table. He quickly sheathed himself and drew her on top of him, dragging her legs up on either side of his hips.

Amy shifted above him, the simple movement causing a groan to rumble in his throat. Slowly, he pushed inside her, burying himself deep in her warmth. Closing her eyes, she let the delicious sensation overwhelm her. For a long time, he didn't move. She looked down at him and found her staring at her.

"What?" she whispered.

"Nothing. I'm just enjoying paradise for a bit longer."

Paradise. That was exactly what this was. The place where life was perfection. Amy leaned forward and dropped a kiss on his lips, her long hair falling around his face. "Maybe I can find a way to extend your stay," she said.

"Actually, I was just thinking of ways I could extend *your* stay," Mal said. "Maybe you should get rid of your hotel room and move into the caboose."

"Caboose?"

"It's a little guesthouse out back. We usually rent it to visiting surfers, but it's empty now. It's close to the water and it's simple, but nice. You don't have to leave right away, do you?"

"No. I'd planned to stay longer if you'd agreed to do the story. But now that you're not interested, I—"

"I'm reconsidering that, too," Mal said. "At least the book idea."

Amy pushed up, staring at him in disbelief. Oh, God,

had the sex been that great? She'd never intended to use her body to get ahead professionally. And yet he'd told her before that he didn't want to participate and now he was wavering. She couldn't take back what had just happened. What was she supposed to do now?

"I suppose I could stay a bit longer," she said. Of course she would. If there was still a chance he wanted to do the story, she'd live in his caboose and spend every moment of her free time with him.

But could she sleep with him again? Amy curled up against his body, resting her head on his shoulder. That was one question that didn't have a clear answer.

3

MAL HAD ENJOYED the company of many different women. And he'd never regretted a single encounter. But there was a tiny bit of doubt that picked at his brain, a thought that maybe his motives for taking Amy to bed weren't as simple as just a pleasurable release.

It was all about expectations. He'd always made it clear to the women in his life that he wasn't ready to settle down to a normal existence. And they in turn realized that a life with an adventure guide was less about love and more about loneliness. Mal wasn't about to put another person through what his mother had experienced. If and when he decided to settle down with one woman, he'd be giving up his globe-trotting ways.

But this. This was a different situation. Taking Amy to bed had certainly satisfied the immediate need that had been coursing through this body. Maybe he'd hoped to drive her away, expecting her to bolt the moment he kissed her. But she hadn't run. Instead, she'd met his desire with a deep and powerful need of her own. Who was this woman? And what was it about Amy Engalls that made him want her so much even when it could only lead to pain in the end?

But he couldn't dwell on all that right now. Losing himself inside her was his only priority. Mal smoothed his hands along her hips and sighed deeply. "So you'll stay?" he murmured, his lips brushing against her ear.

"It might take a bit more convincing," Amy countered.

She set a slow rhythm at first, rocking above him and clearly enjoying the feel of him moving inside of her. Though they barely knew each other, it didn't matter. They were here, together, in this moment, and she wanted him. He was quite willing to oblige.

Mal watched as pleasure suffused her pretty features. She was even more beautiful than she had been in the pub, her pale hair mussed, the color high on her cheeks. He reached out and cupped her breast in his palm, running his thumb across the stiff peak.

From now on, he wouldn't be able to see her as a reporter. She'd be this naked woman straddling his hips, his lover, bringing him indescribable pleasure.

She took him to the edge again and again, then she'd slow her pace or even stop to kiss him. Mal allowed her to have her fun, but it was becoming more difficult to maintain his control.

He reached between them and touched her, running his finger along the damp slit where they were joined. Her second orgasm came almost as quickly as her first, and when her body spasmed around him, Mal gave up control and let his own release take over.

The pleasure seemed to go on forever, wave after wave, until he was completely spent. It was a deep exhaustion, the kind he experienced after a long day of climbing or a hard run. But with this woman in his bed, he realized the exhaustion would only be temporary. They had the rest of the evening to explore each other's desires.

Amy looked down at him, her eyes sleepy, her expression satisfied. "That was nice," she said with a naughty smile.

"Are you going to write about that?"

"Yes," she teased. "I've always wanted a career in erotica."

"Make sure you get the details right. I want everyone to know how good I am."

"Oh, but we'd have to keep your identity anonymous. I wouldn't want all the women of the world chasing after you, trying to get into your bed."

"So you'd get all the glory and I'd get none of the benefits. Is that how it would go?" He pulled her down beside him, pulling her leg over his hip and holding it there. "I'm not promising anything."

"I understand," she said. "That's not why I let you take me to bed."

"Why did you?" Mal asked, suddenly curious.

"I guess I wanted to do something reckless. I'm always so careful and I've never lived on the edge or taken big risks. And this felt…dangerous." She shrugged. "That sounds kind of silly, doesn't it?"

"Not at all. It felt dangerous to me, too."

"You climb mountains and cross glaciers. How could having sex with me be dangerous?"

"I don't ever want to get out of this bed," Mal admitted. "I'd be satisfied to stay here for the next month or two."

"I could be like a sexual expedition," Amy suggested. "We could get some freeze-dried food and set up a camp stove in the corner over there. We'd just camp out until we've both had enough."

"That's not a bad idea," he said.

"But I'm only here for two weeks," Amy said. "Then I have to go home."

Mal sat up, bracing his arm on the mattress. "If you want a story, I'll give you a story. Not the one you came here for, but something interesting. I'll take you down to the Southern Alps and we'll do our own little expedition. You can write about it and maybe your editor will want to buy it."

"What kind of trip?" Amy asked.

"We're putting together a beginner's package, teaching basic mountaineering skills. We'll walk across the Bonar Glacier and climb Mount French. It would be better as a summer trip, but if the weather is decent, it's a good trip year round. I'll use you as my test subject and you can write about it. 'A Beginner's Guide to Guided Adventure.'"

"But our magazine doesn't cater to beginners," Amy said.

"Then sell the story someplace else."

"How much is this going to cost?"

"Nothing. I'll do it for free. I need to put together an itinerary anyway, and you can tell me what I'm doing right and wrong. It'll be fun."

"I've never climbed a mountain. Or walked across a glacier. The closest I've ever come to a dangerous trek was walking in Central Park after dark. And I don't have any gear."

"We provide everything," he said.

"Condoms, too?"

Mal chuckled. "Everything."

"Can I think about it?"

"Sweetheart, I'll show you a good time. I can promise you that."

"You already have," Amy said. "Why would you do this?"

"Truth?"

"Always."

"We could really use the publicity," he said. "And if there's a chance that *High Adventure* might pick up the story, then I'm willing to give that a shot."

"You know, they'd definitely pick up the story if it was about your father."

"Tearing apart my family's past wouldn't be helpful for anyone."

"I wouldn't do it that way," she said. "It would be… respectful."

"Let me ask you this. Are you agreeing to go on this trip because you hope you can change my mind?" Mal asked.

"No," Amy said. "If you don't want to talk to me about your father, then I won't bring it up again. I promise. But if you do bring it up again, then I reserve the right to try to convince you. I still believe it would be a good for you, your business and your family. And I'm not going to change my mind on that."

"All right," Mal said. "We agree to disagree on that. We'll leave tomorrow."

"Tomorrow? That soon? Don't I have to…prepare?"

"Yes. I'd recommend having as much sex as possible. I always recommend that."

"To all your clients?"

"No, I never bonk my clients. I have rules, and that's a hard and fast one."

"And reporters aren't supposed to bonk their subjects."

"You're not a client and I'm not your subject."

"But I'm going to be a client," Amy said. "Or at least, I'm going to pretend to be."

"Not a paying client. And you're going to write about yourself, not me. So we've managed to take care of all the rules. At least the important ones."

"There are others?"

"No whinging. No getting all wobbly if I push you to do something. This won't be a tiki tour, this is going to be hard work."

"Hard yakka," Amy said.

"Yes."

"I have no idea what I'm agreeing to, but it *sounds* reasonable."

"And you won't pike out if the going gets tough?"

"I won't pike out. As long as *piking* means give up. If it doesn't, then I'm not sure."

"That's what it means," Mal said.

"I'm excited. I've never been on an adventure."

"Why not? Your father and brother are always taking trips. You've never gone with them?"

Amy shook her head. "My parents divorced when I was ten, before my dad started adventuring. My brother was sixteen. He decided to live with my dad and that's what they did together." She paused. "Could I die climbing this mountain?"

"You can die crossing the street," he said.

"Answer my question."

"Not likely. You'll be with me and I'm an excellent guide. I'll keep you safe."

"And warm," she said. "I don't like to be cold."

"And warm." Mal pulled her closer. "Are you cold right now?"

"No," she said. "But if you wanted, you could warm me up."

Mal growled softly. "I'm working for tips. I suppose I ought to oblige."

"I'll give you a tip," Amy whispered. "Let me do the story."

"You're not going to give up, are you?"

"No. But I will promise not to bug you incessantly. And I'll give you another tip."

"What's that?"

"I really like it when you kiss my neck."

"Anything else?"

"Next time, you should be on top."

"That can definitely be arranged," he said.

"Taste it."

Amy wrinkled her nose as she squinted down at the plate, Mal's version of bringing her food in bed. "Is that chocolate? On toast?"

"Nope. Go ahead. This is a staple of the Kiwi diet. It's also the only thing I have left in the house to eat. The bread was in the freezer. After a month away, I need to make a trip to the Pak'nSave."

She picked up the bread and sniffed it, then shook her head. It smelled awful. Like…yeast. "I know what that is. It's…Mermite."

"Marmite. And this is actually Vegemite. It's pretty much the same thing, but I prefer Vegemite."

"You're sure this is the only thing to eat in the house? You don't have any cookies or ice cream? Maybe some potato chips?"

"I have a can of smoked oysters and some crackers, a can of tuna and three packages of freeze-dried mac and cheese that expired a year ago."

Amy shoved the plate back at him. "I'd rather try the mac and cheese." She grabbed the sheet from the bed and wrapped it around her naked body. "Come on, show me your kitchen and I'll make us something. I may not be able to climb a mountain, but I can navigate a kitchen."

He pulled her back onto the mattress. "Can I just tell you that I find cooking skills very sexy?"

"I'm famished," she cried.

Grudgingly, Mal got out of bed and followed her into the kitchen, tugging on a pair of boxer shorts along the way. Though Amy had never cooked with a half-naked man, she tried her best to focus on the supper preparations. Mal leaned against the counter, watching her.

She opened up cabinets, pulling out packages that seemed promising. Then she went to the refrigerator. It was nearly empty. She found a shriveled onion in the vegetable bin along with a bag of carrots that still looked edible and a stick of butter. "How old are these eggs?"

"At least a month," Mal said as he munched on the Vegemite sandwich. "No older than two months."

The expiry date on the package said they were still fine, so she placed them on the counter. She pulled out a bowl from the cupboard and set it beside the eggs, then picked up a package of freeze-dried vegetables. "How do I make these?"

"Just run some hot water into the bag and let them sit for five minutes." He studied her as she moved around the kitchen. "You live in New York?"

"Yes."

"Right in the city?"

Amy nodded. "Not in Manhattan. In Brooklyn. Have you ever been to New York?"

"I've seen it from a plane. The Statue of Liberty is pretty cool. But I'm not much for big cities. Too claustrophobic. I like to be able to see the horizon."

"What made you decide to follow in your father's footsteps?" Amy asked.

His brow shot up. "Is this on the record?"

"No," she said, glancing over at him. "I'm just curious. I'll tell you when it's on the record."

Mal shrugged. "I think it was a way to get closer to him," he said. "My brothers and I used to camp and hike when we were younger and we'd talk about our dad and some of the adventures he had. He was a superhero to us, and I guess we wanted to be like him. To my mum's dismay. She isn't happy about what we do, but we're all much more careful than my father."

"He wasn't careful?"

"He enjoyed living on the edge," Mal said. "Climbing was a religious experience to him. He used to say that adrenaline fed his soul. It's not the same for me. I like being outdoors, I like helping people see places that not everyone gets to see. But for me, I started climbing to figure out who my father was and why he did it."

"What about your brothers?"

"I'm not sure. I've never asked them why they do it. I just assumed it was for the same reasons." He drew a deep breath. "It feels good to talk about him. He seems more real when I do, not just some vague memory."

"He was a legend," she said.

"Yeah. But that may have been more of a curse for him than a blessing. Maybe if he hadn't had to live up to his own myth, he might have been more careful."

"And now he's left you to live up to him."

"I try not to dwell on that. It only makes me feel as though I haven't done enough. His business was made on his reputation. I don't have that advantage."

"Believe me, I understand. My father is a bit mythical himself. He's constantly trying to challenge me, throwing rocks in the road and hoping I fail."

"How?"

"He gave me a job at an adventure magazine when I would have been happy writing about shoes or purses. Or even casseroles and oven mitts. He was sure I'd quit, but then I started to like the job. And I'm really good at what I do."

"You're good at other things too," Mal teased. "I can testify to that."

They continued to chat about his childhood, about the move from Australia back to his mother's family in New Zealand, the difficulties of dealing with his father's death and the financial fallout. Amy was surprised at how easily he opened up, especially about his mother's battle with Roger Innis.

That part of the story hadn't been in her research. It was something that both parties had kept private. But from what Mal told her, his father's partner had written a partnership agreement that was very favorable to him.

And one that had left Maxwell Quinn's wife and four children with almost nothing. Mal's mother had always worked, but after Max's death, her income had been barely enough to support the family. They'd relied on his father's income as a guide and corporate sponsorships.

Amy grabbed a pair of plates from the cupboard next to the sink. "I've heard Innis has talked about mounting an expedition to Everest to bring down your father's body."

"I know. It would be almost impossible. But he's getting publicity, appearing to be the good guy. I wish he'd just naff off and leave our family in peace."

She nodded, then slid half the omelet onto his plate. "Then you should say that," Amy said, handing him the plate. "Publicly. The climbing community needs to know that you don't want your father disturbed. Make Innis look like the…the bugger he is."

"Bludger," Mal said. "Bugger is something entirely different."

"Bludger," she repeated as she handed him a fork.

Mal dug into the omelet, then smiled as he got his first taste. "Good on ya. Who would have thought to make an omelet stuffed with mac and cheese?"

"And freeze-dried veggies," she said. "In my opinion, you can put almost anything in an omelet and, as long as the eggs are cooked well, it will taste good."

"Even Vegemite?" he said.

"All right, almost anything."

"Just imagine what you could do with real food," he said. "If you can cook a decent steak I might have to lock you up and never let you go."

"I can," Amy said. "But pasta is my specialty. And I make killer brownies."

"I love brownies," he said, as he gobbled down the omelet. "Maybe we should stay here and you can just cook for me for the next week. The only time I get a decent meal is at my mum's place. I usually lose at least a stone when I'm gone for a month eating freeze-dried food."

"How much is a stone?"

"Around six kilos."

"How much is that in pounds?"

Mal calculated silently. "Around thirteen, I think?"

She took a bite of her food and nodded. "I suppose we could always wait a few days before we leave and I can fatten you up."

"It will take that long to get our gear together. And I have to arrange for the helicopter. Our pilot might not be available on such short notice. So what are you going to make for breakfast? I'll go out and get you anything you need."

"Hold it. Back up, there. What helicopter?"

"The one that will drop us at the edge of the glacier. That's where we'll set up our first camp and I'll teach you how to walk in crampons. We'll get you accustomed to the ice. And then we'll walk across the glacier."

"I've never been in a helicopter," she murmured. In truth, she'd never been very comfortable with heights.

It took all her courage to get on plane, but a helicopter was a totally different thing.

But she couldn't pass up this opportunity because of some silly fear, she chided herself. People flew in helicopters every day and they survived. "Great. That should be fun."

"I can guarantee you'll have fun," he assured her.

"And what do I get in return for my skills as a chef?"

He set his empty plate on the counter next to him, then jumped off. "All the sex you want. Multiple orgasms. And a naked man in your bed willing to do whatever you ask of him."

"It's your bed," she said.

"Don't quibble over details," he murmured, kissing her slowly.

Amy drew back and speared a piece of her omelet, holding it out in front of his nose. Mal opened his mouth and she fed it to him.

"Can you make pancakes?" he asked.

"Blueberry, chocolate chip or plain?"

"All three," he said. He grabbed her waist and pulled her along with him toward the bedroom.

"Where are we going?"

"I need to start working up a credit balance," he said. "I'm really hungry."

4

SHE WAS FREAKING out, Mal realized. Amy stood in the conference room at Maximum Adrenaline, staring at the pile of gear spread across the wide table. Mal draped his arm around her shoulders and pulled her close, pressing a kiss to the top of her head.

"I'm going to wear all this clothing?"

"No," Mal said. "You should have a base layer, a fleece layer and an outerwear layer. This is just a selection of the smaller sizes that we have. Start with the base layer. I think the dark blue ones will probably work. If not those, try the gray. The fit should be close to your skin, but not overly tight."

"Won't I need a change of clothing?"

"Just an extra base and fleece layer to sleep in. You'll carry that in your pack, along with lots of socks. I'll see if I can find you a pair of boots." Mal reached in his pocket and pulled out a pair of sunnies, then slipped them onto the bridge of Amy's nose. "You'll need those. The snow can be really bright under the sun."

He turned and walked out of the room, heading

for the storage shed where they kept their gear. Dana watched him pass her desk then hurried after him, Duffy at her heels. When they got outside, she fell into stride next to him. "What are you doing?"

"I'm prepping for a trip."

"I mean with her. She's a reporter, Mal. She came here to get a story."

"It's not like that," he replied. "We have an agreement. Nothing I say to her is on the record unless she says it is."

"Did you lose your mind in Greenland?"

"We're friends. I trust her."

"Why? You don't even know her."

That was true, Mal had to admit. But they'd shared some very intimate moments, moments where they'd both exposed their vulnerabilities. He'd rarely had time for women and had never had anything that resembled a real relationship. His job came first. But with Amy, he almost felt...normal. It wasn't just about the sex, even though the sex was great. They *talked* to each other and she understood him.

Sure, there was a chance he could be fooling himself, but Mal had lived by his instincts for long enough to be confident that Amy wouldn't betray him. If he knew anything about Amy, it was that she couldn't hide her true feelings. Her every emotion was written across her face the moment she felt it.

Dana grabbed his arm and pulled him to a stop. "You have lost your mind. And when she splashes our whole story on the pages of *High Adventure,* I'm going to say 'I told you so.'" She observed him shrewdly. "Are you— Oh, no. Oh, bloody hell, Mal. No, no, no. You're sleeping with her?"

"No," Mal lied.

"Yes," she said.

"I'm taking her on this trip so she can write about the expedition, and not about our father. I'm not going to even mention Dad. If she can get this story into *High Adventure,* then it will all be worth it. We need the exposure. And I have to put an expedition plan together before we offer this trip to actual paying customers anyway."

"And that's why you're sleeping with her? So she'll get us some free publicity?"

"No!" Mal said. "I'm sleeping with her because she's funny and sweet and hot. It just happened, and now it keeps happening and I don't want to stop it. And who put you in charge of my sex life?"

"You want to stop it? That's easy. Just keep your damn trousers zipped."

"You're starting to sound like Mum," he said.

Dana gasped. "You've said a lot of dodgy things to me in my life, Mal, but that's the worst. I do not sound like Mum."

"I know what I'm doing," Mal said. "I have everything under control."

"Right," Dana replied.

"I do. I'm going to give Amy the trip of a lifetime and that will be it. She goes home in six days."

"Just be careful," Dana warned.

"This is an easy expedition," he said. "No real danger."

"Not the expedition," she said. "Be careful with her."

"Are you finished sticking your nose into my business?"

"Our business," she said. "The family business."

Mal shook his head as he continued on to the equipment shed.

It was a risk. Maybe Amy *was* just a very skilled reporter, adept at getting the truth out of him without raising his suspicions. Hell, maybe his doubts weren't even about the story, Mal mused. Maybe he just wanted to get them both out of his bed. It had only been a few days, but he'd already wasted more than a few minutes thinking about what his life could be like if she was around for more than just two weeks. Any more time together under the sheets and his career, his very existence, would be in serious jeopardy.

So he'd take her on this trip, in six days she would be gone and his life would go back to the way it should be.

Mal found a couple pairs of boots in her size and started back to the office. When he opened the door to the conference room, he found Amy standing amongst the clothes, wearing just her bra and panties, a pair of fleece pants clutched in her hand.

"What's the problem?"

She held up the pants. "Base layer or fleece? And do I wear the fleece over the base layer or instead of the base layer?"

"That depends on the weather," he said. "Sometimes, during the day, it could be warm enough in the sun that you could hike topless."

"Women do that?"

"Sure," he said.

She frowned. "Isn't there some mountain we could

climb in Tahiti or Bora Bora? Someplace where it's warm?"

He bent over and picked up a few pieces of base layer and held them out. "That sounds a lot like whinging, and you promised there would be none of that."

"I don't even know what that means."

"Whining? Complaining?"

"I've never done something like this before and it worries me," Amy admitted.

"You don't have to be afraid, Amy."

"I'm not afraid. I just don't want to make a fool out of myself. I mean, I don't even know the most basic things. For example, what happens when I need to go to the bathroom?"

"Oh, that's easy. There are petrol stations every few miles along the trail, we just stop in and ask for the key."

Amy giggled. "Funny."

He picked up the pants and showed her the waistband. "This opens, you tug down your fleece and base, grab a squat, and Bob's your uncle."

"Bob's my uncle," she murmured. "Yes, he is. I understand the mechanics. But you just…do it? Wherever?"

"Pretty much," he said.

"Just promise me you're not going to watch," she said.

"Your naked bum? I'm sure I'll get plenty of other chances to observe your backside." Mal pulled her into his arms and gave her a lazy kiss. She was cute this way, all nervous and vulnerable.

"And would Bob have any toilet paper along?"

"Yes, we'll take some. But we'll have to carry it back out. There are no trash cans on the glacier."

"All right," she said. "If that's the worst I'll have to deal with, then I'll survive."

"It'll be great, I promise. Now, would you like me to help you into your clothes or out of those knickers?"

"Your sister is right outside the door," she said.

"So?"

"Keep your hands to yourself," Amy warned.

"All my rellies and friends know I'm not a virgin," he said.

"But they don't know I'm having sex with you," she said. He smiled and Amy's eyes went wide. "They do?"

"My sister does. But then, she's always been the nosy one in the family."

Amy grabbed up the bottoms from the base layer and tugged them over her legs. Mal set the boots on the table and watched as she yanked the top over her head. "There. How is that?"

"You look very...sexy."

She found a set of fleece and put those on next. When she was finished, she did a slow circle. "And how's this?"

"I prefer you naked," he commented.

Amy chose a bright blue jacket and black pants. When she was fully dressed, she did another little turn. She looked completely adorable. "Now, that is nice. You're starting to look the part."

She bent her arms up in a muscular pose. "I'm ready for the mountain," she said in a gruff voice.

"Now we have to weigh your pack," he said. "Come on, I have it outside."

Amy walked to the door. "Is it really going to be so cold that I'll need all these layers?"

"No, not all the time. But if we run into bad weather, it's better to be prepared. It *is* winter and the days are a lot shorter."

They walked outside, where Mal had laid out the equipment on the porch. "All right, you're going to have clothing, food and gear in your pack. A sleeping bag and pad. I'll carry the tent and the stove. Do you know what this stuff is?" he asked, pointing to a collection of climbing tools.

Amy nodded, walking along the row. "Climbing harness. Helmet. These are carabineers and these are Prusiks." She named the other items and then turned to him, waiting for confirmation.

"Good," he said. "Now let's get you into the harness and get that adjusted and then we'll put all this in your pack."

They spent the next fifteen minutes getting in and out of the harness, made much more difficult by the layers of clothes. Amy ended up flat on the ground twice and Mal patiently pulled her up to her feet. He was usually all business when it came to trip prep, but this was fun. They laughed and kissed and rolled around on the grass until he questioned the wisdom of taking the trip at all.

He could have fun with Amy anywhere. She made him laugh with just a silly expression or a goofy comment. And every time he looked at her or touched her, she seemed more beautiful.

Seven days just wasn't enough time. Not for everything he wanted to do. The thought of letting her walk out of his life, even now, was painful to consider.

But they existed on separate continents. And in his life there was no place for a woman. Making it work was impossible.

"All right, I'm ready for the pack," Amy said.

"This is fifteen kilos," he said. "It's probably going to be a bit too heavy."

"I can do it," Amy said.

"If it is, I'll take some of the weight in my pack."

"No, I want to do it."

Mal added the climbing gear, then hefted the pack up and helped her slip the straps over her shoulders. He let go slowly, but the weight pulled her back and she began to fall. Mal grabbed for her hands, but she only brought him down on top of her.

"I think it might be too heavy," she said with a giggle.

"Maybe we should just stay in bed. It's a lot less work."

"What will I have to write about then?"

"Oh, I'm sure we could suss out something exciting. You could sell it as an erotic novel."

THEY SPENT THE night before their departure cooking a lavish steak dinner and talking about the adventure ahead. Amy was confident she could handle the pack and Mal had assured her that the trip wasn't going to be difficult for someone who was reasonably fit. Still, Amy was well aware of her track record on adventures. Was she only setting herself up for failure?

"What is it?"

She looked across the table to find him watching her. "Nothing," she said. "I just have a lot to remember."

He held out his hand and wiggled his fingers. "Grab your wine. Let's go for a walk."

The night was chilly and he wrapped her in a bulky sweater, then slipped into his own jacket. They walked down to the sand and stared out at the sea. The night sky was filled with stars, and a tiny sliver of moon hung over the horizon.

She sat on a weathered beach chair, tucking her feet up under her, as Mal built a fire. When the flames licked at the wood, he sat back on his heels. Amy got up and knelt behind him, wrapping her arms around his neck.

"My dad used to build these amazing campfires with us."

"He took you camping?"

"Yeah. Just me and the twins. My mum stayed with us during the day, but she'd go home with Dana at night. She didn't like sleeping in a tent."

"That must have been fun, to spend time with just your dad and brothers," Amy said.

She was awed by how quickly he'd opened up to her, how easy it had become between them. She thought back to the moment they'd met, to all her worries, all the scenarios that could have played out between them. This was the last thing she could have predicted. Her working vacation had turned into a romantic getaway. And yet the story was still in the back of her mind. She could tell he was considering it.

"You know, I've talked more about my dad in the past week than I have in the twenty years since he died," Mal murmured. "It feels good."

Though Mal had talked about his father, he still refused to address the choices that faced him and his family in regards to Max's body. Amy could understand his reluctance to comment on the media speculation. But his silence would only prolong the interest. She'd make the best of the story if he gave it to her. After all, she was called "The Fixer" around the office, the copy editor who could polish the most uninteresting story into a gleaming gem of adventure writing.

"He must have been a fun guy to be around."

"Sure. When he was around," Mal said. "There are some things I remember so clearly. Things we did together. And though I know he was gone a lot, I don't remember the absences. Our lives just went into a holding pattern, waiting for him to return. And then he'd come home and we'd start living again."

"My father was always gone, too. I thought it was business, but I later found out he had a mistress. He and my mother should have never gotten married."

"Why would you say that?" Mal said. "Then they never would have made you. I can testify to the fact that at least one good thing came from their marriage."

She smiled but it quickly faded. "Do you wonder if we'll ever stop trying to live up to our parents' expectations? Look at me. My father still controls my life—at least my professional life."

"And I'm trying to please a ghost," Mal said, nodding. "I wonder what I might have done with my life if my father had been a postman or a schoolteacher. Would I have followed in his footsteps then? Would I have considered that life exciting and fulfilling?"

"We don't have to be defined by our parents' pasts.

I think we all have our own destinies," Amy said. "And we do what we're meant to do." She rested her chin on his shoulder. "For example, you live in New Zealand and I live in New York, and yet we still met. Destiny."

"I can't imagine you living in the city."

"After spending time here, I'm beginning to wonder why I do. I can't imagine you in New York. All that steel and concrete."

Mal poked at the fire with a long stick. "And here I was considering spending a little more time in New York."

Amy sat down beside him in the sand and tried to make out his features in the flicker of light from the flames. He'd been caught up in his thoughts all evening long, not his usual witty self.

"You said we all have our own destinies. But do you ever wonder whether you might have taken the wrong road in life? Whether there might be something else you're meant to do?"

"All the time," Amy said.

He turned to meet her gaze. "Yeah?"

"I didn't set out to be the best copy editor in the world. I wanted to run one of my father's magazines. In truth, I wanted to run his whole magazine group. But now I realize that sitting in an office correcting someone else's work isn't really the life I want." She drew a deep breath. "This is my kind of life. Staring at the stars, sitting by the fire."

"See? You're hooked already."

She bumped against his shoulder. "I think I am. So have we covered everything that I need to know before we leave?"

"There is one rule that we haven't discussed," he said. He smoothed his hand over her cheek and brushed his lips across hers.

"Another rule?"

"This one is very important," he murmured. "Crucial."

"What is it?"

"You must do everything I tell you to do. No questions, no whinging. From the minute we head out, you're my responsibility and I take that seriously."

"All right," Amy said. "Maybe we should practice that. We've practiced everything else."

"How are we going to practice?"

She pushed to her feet and stood between him and the fire. "Order me to do something."

He shook his head. "All right. If you insist. Kiss me. And make it good."

Amy laughed. "I was thinking you might send me for firewood."

"We have plenty of firewood."

Grudgingly, she leaned forward and touched her lips to his. But when she tried to draw away, he slipped his hand around her nape and pulled her in, his mouth covering hers in a demanding assault. Her body reacted immediately and Amy moaned softly. Suddenly, he let her go and she stepped back.

"Now take your clothes off," he said.

"Here? It's freezing out."

"It's not even close to freezing. You're about to hike out on a glacier. If you're not ready for the cold, I need to know now."

"Are we planning to do the trek naked?" Amy asked.

"Are you questioning my orders?" Mal countered.

Amy reached for the front of her sweater, then shrugged it off her shoulders. He took a seat on the beach chair, reclining out and observing her silently as she discarded each piece of clothing.

Amy wasn't sure if this was part of some grand seduction or if he was testing her, but she was determined to meet the challenge. A damp breeze blew off the water and she shivered, her skin prickling with goose bumps.

The fire was warm on her back and she closed her eyes and tipped her face up to the night sky, running her hands through her hair. When she met his eyes again, she noticed desire burning in the blue depths. Two could play this game, Amy mused.

"How's this?" she asked, smoothing her hands over her breasts and letting them rest on her belly. "No whinging."

"Turn around," he said in a ragged voice.

She did as she was told, reaching over her shoulder to twist her hair around her fingers. Amy could almost feel his gaze admiring her silhouette. She hadn't even touched him, and yet she sensed the need pulsing between them. She wasn't cold at all. Her body was flushed with warmth, her heart beating a swift rhythm in her chest.

She sensed him behind her before she felt his hands on her shoulders. When he smoothed his palms along her bare arms, Amy leaned back into his body.

Every nerve was tingling as he moved his hands forward and caressed her breasts. Her nipples were taut and aching for the damp of his tongue. His hands drifted lower, finding the sensitive spot between her legs. Amy reached back and wove her fingers through his thick hair.

"Tell me you want me," he whispered, his breath hot against her ear.

Was this the guide talking or her lover? Amy didn't care. The sensations racing through her were enough to make her say anything that might result in her release. "I want you," she said.

He yanked her against him, then scooped her up in his arms. Amy cried out in surprise, but as he started toward the house, she relaxed and nuzzled her face into his shoulder, sucking gently.

As soon as they were through the front door, Mal put her on her feet again, then trapped her against the wall, his lean body pressed against hers. He was already hard. Amy unzipped his pants and tugged aside his boxers. When she wrapped her fingers around his stiff shaft, a strangled "yes" slipped from his throat.

They were too lost in their need to make it to the bedroom, or to fetch a condom. This wasn't about a slow, lazy exploration, but about intense pleasure and immediate release.

His lips never left hers as they brought each other closer to the edge. She stroked the length of his shaft, increasing her tempo as she began to lose touch with reality. It was a desperate climb to the top, both of them caught inside their own fantasies.

When they finally reached the summit, amid breathless pleas and delicious moans, it was the perfect end. Her hand was slick with his heat and she was wet with her own. They collapsed against the wall, his arm wrapped around her waist.

"Crikey dick, that was amazing," he muttered.

The silly slang made her laugh and, already too weak to stand, she slipped down to the floor, dragging him along with her. They sat against the wall, Amy completely naked and Mal fully dressed except for his unzipped jeans.

Amy had never been a dedicated fan of sex. But Mal was changing that. A great part of her day was spent wondering when they'd toss aside their clothes and enjoy themselves. But she'd never thought that it would reach that level of desperation. "I followed orders," she said.

"You certainly did," he said.

"Crikey dick?"

"It just came out."

"Please don't say that again. Especially after sex."

"Who's giving the orders now?"

"It's just a request. 'Holy shit' would probably be more appropriate."

"Okay, boss."

"Boss?"

"I've decided to make you the boss when it comes to sex. I'll take care of the rest."

"Oh, goody," Amy said. She struggled to get to her feet, then stood above him. "Lose the clothes. Now."

Mal sent her a wicked smile. "Don't abuse your power, bugalugs. I might take it back."

"Just try," she said. Amy turned and walked toward the bedroom, letting her hips sway provocatively.

With a low curse, Mal crawled after her, groaning. "You're a cruel woman, Amy Engalls."

"YOU'RE AS BRIGHT as a box of budgies."

Amy glanced over at Mal and forced a smile. They'd made the commercial flight from Auckland to Christchurch early that morning. They were due to meet the helicopter in less than a half hour at a small cluster of hangars near the south end of the airport. The closer they got to departure, the more forced Amy's cheer became.

Mal knew she wasn't looking forward to the flight. She'd been jumpy enough on the jet. But he hoped that once she got used to it, she'd have a chance to appreciate the scenery below them. Rick Mulligan, the pilot, was an old friend and had worked for Mal on many occasions. Normally, he got paid, but for this trip, Mal was calling in a favor. Frequent flyer miles had paid for the commercial flight and for Rick, Mal had agreed to barter a trek for him and his groomsmen as a bachelor party activity in return for the helicopter flight.

"You'll like it," Mal said. "I promise. If you don't I'll—"

"Refund the money I've paid you?" she asked.

He chuckled. "No, I'll find a way to make it up to you. But this way, you're going to witness some of the most beautiful landscapes in the world in the course of a few hours. It's the best way to see New Zealand."

He slipped his hand into his jacket pocket and withdrew a small package. "I bought something for you."

She frowned. "You got me a present? Oh, God, is this ride going to be that bad?"

"It's just something I thought we should have for the trip."

"It's too small for toilet paper." Amy unwrapped the

package and when she saw what was inside, she smiled. "A digital camera."

"You'll want to document your trip for the article, and you should start with the ride into the glacier. And this camera takes really nice photos. High res. It's small enough to string around your neck but the buttons are easy to work with gloves on. I have one just like it."

"Thank you," she said. Amy leaned across the seat and kissed his cheek. "I'm going to write a really good story."

"Aren't you biased if you've already decided how well it's going to go? What about your journalistic integrity? What if it's a bad trip?"

"It's not going to be a bad trip," she said. "Please, don't make it a bad trip. I don't want to have to write anything negative about you."

"Don't worry. I'm going to show you what you're made of."

She turned away, and the rest of the drive was spent in silence. Mal had dealt with insecure clients in the past, but he'd always looked at it as part of his job. Amy wasn't a client, she was… Bloody hell, what was she? His lover? His temporary companion? There wasn't really a name for the kind of relationship they shared.

They'd been too intimate to be considered acquaintances and yet had never professed any deep emotional attachment to each other beyond sexual desire and apparent affection. He shouldn't care that there were no words to describe it.

But she made him think. Until now, his only priority had been making the family business more successful than Roger Innis's company and making his own mark on the adventure world. He secretly celebrated when weather prevented Innis's summit bids, or when his clients complained about the service on internet forums. He told himself that it was karma for everything that Innis had done wrong the night Mal's father had died.

Only after enjoying Amy's company the past couple of days, he wondered if he'd cheated himself of some of the pleasures of life. Suddenly, trumping Innis didn't seem as important as it once had. He couldn't put his finger on the reason. Maybe it was because his every waking hour was occupied with thoughts of Amy; he just hadn't had time to focus on business concerns.

But was it more than just simple distraction? Had she somehow managed to penetrate the wall he'd built up around his heart?

From the moment he'd first set foot on a mountainside, Mal had known that his life would be spent in the single-minded pursuit of adventure. He'd also conceded that this would allow little time for a personal life, and no time for a wife and kids. But he'd been more than willing to make the sacrifice. He'd never wanted a family.

And now? All he knew was that he wanted…more. More than just an endless itinerary of treks and expeditions, long hours in airports and cold nights in tiny tents. He wanted something that still remained nameless, a vague, unfocused thing that he suspected might make him happier than he'd ever been. Was it love?

Mal drew in a deep breath. No. He wasn't ready to admit that. He had great affection for Amy, but love? They'd just met. And they lived in different worlds. And for Mal, love was an impossibility, something only available to other men who led boring lives. He wouldn't put a woman and children through the same anxiety and pain that his mother and siblings had gone through.

The taxi turned onto the road that led to the private hangars. As they approached the cluster of metal buildings, he saw the helicopter, sitting near one of the hangars. Rick waved as they stopped. Mal hopped out and shook Rick's hand and then helped Amy out of the cab. He paid the driver and moved to unload their gear.

"Rick Mulligan, this is Amy Engalls. Amy, Rick, our pilot."

"I've never been in a helicopter before," she blurted out. "Are they really safe?"

"I've been flying them for almost fifteen years and I'm still here. I take meticulous care of my birds. You're in excellent hands."

They unloaded all the gear and stowed it in the cargo trays attached to the struts of the helicopter before taking a few photos. Then Mal got Amy settled in her seat and put the headphones over her ears. For good measure, he gave her a quick kiss, something that didn't go unnoticed by Rick.

"Make it a nice ride," he said when he got his own headphones on.

Rick started the blades spinning and within minutes, they were airborne, hovering for a moment before surging forward. Amy's eyes went wide and she let out a tiny scream. Grabbing her hand, he gave it a gentle squeeze and she covered her eyes with the other.

As Mal had predicted, fifteen minutes into the flight, Amy's fears had vanished and she even risked a look down. He leaned over and pointed out features of the rugged land beneath them.

No matter how many times he'd seen it, it was always breathtaking. But this trip, it took on much more meaning because he wanted Amy to love it, too. Mal wasn't sure why. Maybe he hoped she'd want to come back. Or perhaps it was so she'd understand why he could never leave.

They flew through deep valleys filled with lush forests, then danced along rocky ridges. In the distance, the snow-covered Southern Alps stood against the blue sky. As they rose in altitude, they flew above the tree line and the landscape became more barren and rugged. Jagged rock was visible below them and in the cols and saddles between the peaks, glaciers flowed, massive rivers of ice.

Amy turned and looked at him. "Thank for this. I'm glad you were the one to show me."

Mal leaned over and kissed her, then slipped his fingers through the hair at her nape. For a long moment, they lost themselves in a lazy exploration of lips and tongues. He heard Rick's voice through the headphones and drew away.

"We'll be landing at Bevan Col in a few minutes," the pilot said.

"Here we go," Amy said. She pulled out her camera and took a few photos through the window and then drew a deep breath.

Before long, they were standing on the col, the edge of the glacier visible in the distance, waving goodbye to Rick. They watched the helicopter rise up in front of them, their packs resting on the rocky ground. The sound of the rotating blades faded into the distance as the helicopter disappeared from view.

Mal draped his arm around Amy's shoulders. "Are you all right?"

She nodded. "How far are we from the nearest road?"

"Far," he said.

"Okay." She nodded. "Okay." She sighed deeply. "Okay."

"Can you stop saying that?"

"Okay."

"Why don't we set up camp and make something to eat. We've got a long day ahead of us tomorrow and it's going to be dark in a few hours."

"Okay." She winced. "Sorry. That's a very good idea. How can I help?"

"You can just sit down on your pack and watch. I'll take care of things. That's what the guide is supposed to do."

"No, I want to help," she said. "No whinging, remember?

"All right then, I'll show you how to set up our tent."

"I don't get my own tent?" Amy asked.

"No," Mal replied.

"But I'm the client. I should have my own tent, don't you think?"

"Yes, *if* you were a client. But you're not."

"But I'm pretending to be. And if you'd give a client her own tent, then I should have *my* own."

He unhitched the tent bag from his pack and tossed it at her. "There you go. It's all yours. And you can carry it from now on because that's what a client does when she gets her own tent."

"Where are you going to sleep?" Amy asked.

"Outside. My bag is rated for subzero weather. I'll just toss my pad on the snow and sleep outside."

Amy sent him a smile. "You can always sleep in my tent."

Mal opened his mouth to reply, then snapped it shut. She was testing him, trying to see how patient he really was. "No, I'm fine sleeping on the cold, icy ground. A client should have her privacy. Now dump that bag out and I'll show you how to put your tent together. And no more whinging."

"That wasn't whinging."

"I know whinging when I hear it," Mal said. He nodded to her. "Put that in your little reporter's notes. You can quote me."

Amy dumped the tent onto the ground. "All right, I will. Do you have any other orders, sir?"

"Not at the present," Mal replied.

This was going to be an interesting trip, he mused. In fact, he was glad for it. Mal had seen it a thousand times. When clients were put under the stress of living in extreme conditions, their true personalities came out. He'd never guided a trip where a client was able to complete the expedition without blowing up or melting down at least once. He wondered when it would happen with Amy. And then he'd have proved himself right that this wasn't the life for her.

5

THEY HAD DINNER in the tent, the flap open to take in the view of the sunset over the col. Amy had never witnessed anything so breathtaking. The mountains surrounded them on all four sides, the jagged peaks jutting into the clear blue sky. Though she knew they were small peaks compared to those in the Himalayas, one of them would represent her first climb. And they looked imposing to her.

She drew a deep breath of the crisp, clean air, so different from the smell of bus exhaust and smog that she enjoyed in New York. How different his life was from hers. And yet here she was, learning the ropes. She'd set up the tent with his careful instruction. And he'd showed her how to work the alcohol stove and let her make the meal.

Amy sat cross-legged in front of him, dressed in her fleece, her hat pulled low over her brow. "Does everyone use this freeze-dried food?"

Mal nodded. "There are only a few places that make a decent meal," he said.

"Don't you ever get bored with it?"

"Yeah, but when you're carrying your food around in a pack, you don't want to be dragging ten pounds of steak and potatoes up a mountainside."

"But you could put your own meals together. I copy-edited an article for the magazine on this woman who makes her own freeze-dried meals and then vacuum packs them. I tried some of her stuff and it was much better than this."

"People really don't come for the food," he said. "They come for the scenery."

"Yeah, but if you make the food good, maybe they'll come for both."

"Have you tasted my cooking? They'd probably be more likely to run in the other direction."

"True," Amy said, crawling across the tent. She braced her hands on his knees and kissed him. "Maybe if you could add kissing to the menu, women would forget about the mediocre food."

"What about the men?" he murmured, his lips playfully brushing against hers.

"They'll just have to make do," she replied.

Mal set down his supper, then cupped her face in his warm hands. "Thank you for making dinner."

"I'm getting the hang of this," she said. "And I haven't complained once. I might just be the perfect client. I should get my trip for free," she teased.

But though she teased about it, Amy couldn't help but wonder what this trip was costing him. "How much would you charge for this trip?"

"A couple thousand," he said.

"Plus the helicopter ride. We could have driven in and walked to the glacier."

"That's how we're leaving," Mal said. "Besides, the pilot owed me a favor. He flew us in for free."

Amy smiled. "That was very nice of him to do. And nice of you, too."

She put his supper aside and curled up in his lap. "It's freezing."

He reached up to zip the flap, shutting out the last of the day's light. "I'll keep you warm, I promise." Mal found a small flashlight in the pocket of his jacket and flipped it on. It provided just enough illumination to appreciate his body as he shrugged out of his clothing.

Mal unlaced her boots and set them in the corner of the tent, then helped her out of her fleece. When they were both down to the last layer, he zipped the sleeping bags together and they crawled beneath the soft down.

"Better?" he asked.

"Much," she murmured.

They'd become so familiar with each other that seduction had become an adventure. They wriggled out of the last layer and when they were both naked, he pulled her body against his. "I'm having fun," he said, pressing his forehead to hers. "I haven't had real fun for a long time."

"Your trips aren't fun?"

"They're business. I worry about every little detail, hoping that we're going to make decent money, that we won't have any problems, that everyone will leave happy. I really can't enjoy things myself. But I like this, just the two of us, no worries. Only one person to please."

"And how do you plan to please me?"

"I have my ways." He dived beneath the down sleeping bag and Amy screamed as his lips and tongue found his favorite spots on her body. They were like two cats in a sack, the sleeping bags making it almost impossible to move. So Mal unzipped one side and tossed the top bag off them. The interior of the tent had warmed with their body heat and there was just a slight chill in the air.

"Much better," Mal murmured, his lips coming down on her nipple.

A shiver washed over her and Amy lay back and enjoyed the riot of sensation that raced through her body. Earlier today, she'd been apprehensive, not sure how she was going to handle this trip. She'd never been a risk taker. Watching from the sidelines was usually as close as she got to adventure. Yet, here, with Mal, she seemed to be growing more confident by the second. Maybe she really was her father's daughter.

Besides, if she could seduce a man like Mal, she could certainly climb a tiny little mountain or walk across a chilly glacier. Tomorrow, she'd prove to him that she was the kind of woman who might be his perfect match—in bed and out of it.

But what did that mean? He'd made it clear that she shouldn't imagine a future with him. Just knowing that she could attract a man like Mal would have to be enough. She'd go home and live on that confidence for the rest of her life. And maybe she'd try another adventure.

"What's going through that head of yours?" Mal whispered.

She opened her eyes to find him watching her. Amy

reached out and brushed the hair out of his eyes. "Nothing. Just enjoying what you do to me."

She pulled him on top of her, their hips meeting, his erection hard against her belly. Mal braced his hands on either side of her shoulders and kissed her. His tongue traced the crease of her lips and Amy opened to enjoy his taste and warmth.

They were completely alone on the edge of this glacier, far away from all the bustle of real life. They could be the only two people on the earth, thrown together in this desolate place.

"Is this what you dream about when you're alone in your tent?" Amy asked.

"I will from now on," Mal said.

"Good. I want you to think of me." She kissed him softly. "Close your eyes. Tell me what you'll imagine."

He considered his answer for a bit before saying, "I'll think about how your hair falls around your face when you're moving on top of me. And how I anticipate the moment when you take me into your mouth and how it's almost painful and then the most intense pleasure I've ever felt. And how beautiful your body is when you're just out of the shower, your skin all slick and smelling like soap."

"When have you seen me just out of the shower?" Amy asked.

"Yesterday morning. You thought I was still asleep but I was watching."

"And that's going to do it for you?"

"Every time." He shifted above her. "What about you? What will you remember?"

"This," she said. "You lying on top of me, the weight

of your body heavy on mine." Amy parted her legs and his hips found a spot between them. "And how this feels."

Mal pressed the tip of his shaft against her, slipping inside for a fleeting moment. His breath caught in his throat and he bent his head, his mouth hovering above hers.

Amy wanted to feel him without any barriers between them, but she was well aware of the risks. And so was he. He reached over and grabbed the box of condoms he'd brought and handed them to her.

She sheathed him, smoothing the latex over his shaft. And when he buried himself inside her, he didn't drive forward with the need for release. Instead, he was slow and gentle, his gaze never leaving hers.

Mal dragged her leg up along his hip and he plunged deeper. The position sent a strange current through her and she closed her eyes and focused on the spot where they were joined. His rhythm was smooth and even and Amy felt herself dancing close to the edge. It was a strange sensation, as if she wasn't in control of her reactions.

He shifted again and the intensity of her desire was like an electric shock. And then, out of nowhere, her body spasmed, deep and powerful. Mal stopped, her reaction surprising him. But then she whispered his name and in a single thrust, he took her over the edge.

The rest happened in a blur of pleasure and astonishment. This had never happened to her before, this perfect end to a perfect act. The orgasm seemed to come from deep inside her and it went on forever.

The entire trip had been filled with new experiences, but this was a memory that would never fade from her mind.

And in six days, that was all Amy would have of Mal, too.

"Lesson number one," Mal said, holding up his ice ax. "Arresting a fall."

Amy's eyes went wide. "Have you forgotten that I'm not the most coordinated person? If this trip includes the opportunity to fall, I will do it in spectacular fashion."

"It's not so much *fall* as *slide,*" Mal said. "We'll be walking on a steep pitch, and if you slip you can slide a long way down if you don't have the means to stop yourself. That won't actually happen because I'm going to rope you to me, but you still need to learn to stop yourself. Your second line of defense is your crampons." He pointed to the metal spikes she had strapped to her boots. "If you have too much speed they won't help, but at the start of a slide, they can, if you think quickly."

"Who came up with that name?" Amy asked. "Crampon. It sounds like a feminine hygiene product. Why not just call them spikes or something more…masculine?"

He gave her a scolding look. "This is serious stuff, Amy. No joke. Everything I tell you now might save your life someday. You wanted an adventure, this is what comes with it."

"Yes, sir," she said. She gave him a playful salute and focused her attention on what he was saying.

Mal had taught at least a hundred classes in mountaineering and he had his talking points down pat. But he'd never had such a distracting student. He loved watching her work through each exercise, admiring her pretty face and tempting body. Even with the layers of clothing, he could still admire the sweet curves he'd enjoyed the night before.

Once she'd mastered walking in crampons, roped into her harness, he moved on. "These are your poles," he said. "They'll help with balance, but you'll also use them to test the stability of the snow in front of you. We haven't had a lot of snow yet this year, but you never know when you'll come across a crevasse in the ice."

"You have crevasses on this glacier?" she asked.

"There are crevasses on every glacier. This one is pretty well tramped so we'll probably be able to see them, but the danger is always there."

"Great," she muttered. "If I don't fall down the mountain, I'll fall *into* the mountain."

Mal couldn't help but laugh. He knew he ought to keep a professional demeanor, but she did manage to keep this experience interesting. He'd always taught very serious students, those who hoped someday to make summit bids on some of the world's highest mountains. Amy was a novice and would probably stay a novice for the rest of her life. There would be no Mount Everests in her future.

"There is one more thing," he said.

"Oh, good. Another way I can kill myself on this little holiday. Do tell."

"Avalanches." Mal reached down into his pack and handed her an avalanche transponder. "Clip this to your jacket. At the very first hint of an avalanche, reach for it and turn it on."

"Will there be an avalanche? You said there wasn't a lot of snow."

"The chances are slim, but it could happen. And even a small slide can catch you up." He showed her how the transponder worked and they practiced using her shovel to dig through the snow. By the end of the lesson, she was breathless and a little stressed.

He fetched a bottle of water and sat down next to her in the snow. "You're doing well," he said.

Amy took a sip of the water. "You're a good teacher," she replied. Pulling her knees up beneath her chin, she gazed up at the peaks above them. "They look so far away from here. Which one are we going to climb?"

He pointed and she followed the direction of his finger. "That one, just to the right of the big one, which is called Mount Aspiring. Someday I'll take you up there. We're going up Mount French. It has a really nice view. And right over there is a spot we call the Quarterdeck. It's wide and flat and kind of overlooks the whole area. We'll leave our packs there when we go to the summit and pick them up on our way down."

She sat silently for a long time and Mal wondered what worry was going through her head. "So is it the crevasses or the avalanches?" he finally asked.

"Both," she said.

"I wouldn't have brought you up here if I thought it was dangerous," he said. "I'm just teaching you what you might need to know. Like teaching you how avoid a shark attack. You'll swim in lots of places that won't have sharks, but at some point in your life, the information might come in handy. Do you have any questions?"

"What if we both get swept away by the avalanche? Or we both fall in the crevasse?"

He pulled her down into the snow, stretching out on top of her. "That's not going to happen. I promise. I don't want you to spend this trip worrying about the all the disasters that could happen and miss all the beauty in front of you."

"All right," she murmured. She reached up and brushed the hair out of his eyes. "I can do this."

"Of course you can."

She nodded, but he saw a glimmer of a tear in her eye. Was she really that afraid? Or was there something else bothering her? He'd warned her that he wouldn't tolerate whinging, but he didn't want her to keep her fears bottled up inside of her.

"If you're afraid, we can talk about it."

"I'm not afraid," she snapped.

Her reaction startled him at first. He'd never really heard Amy say a cross word to him, or lash out in anger. She was always so even tempered. Maybe she was just tired. They hadn't gotten much sleep last night.

"We can take a nap if you're weary."

"No," Amy insisted. "I don't need a nap. I'm not tired and I'm not afraid."

The way she was glaring at him, with a stubborn tilt to her chin, signaled that he'd better move on. The truth would come out sooner or later. Amy wasn't the best at keeping her feelings a secret.

Even now, with anger and stubbornness clouding her features, there was something about the way she looked at him that he loved. She saw him as something more than just a climber, more than a guy who lived on the edge and cheated death every day. Though she respected what he did, Amy focused more on the simple things—quiet conversation, a night wrapped in each other's arms, breakfast together in the morning. Even a little argument. The day-to-day happenings that made a relationship function. They barely talked about climbing or his work. She was more interested in the books he'd read and the music he liked.

Was that what his father had found attractive about his mother? His mum had never set foot on a mountainside. She wasn't interested in adventure. She'd wanted to make a home.

Mal didn't remember much about them as a couple, as the time his father had spent with Mal and his brothers remained foremost in his memories. But he did remember their laughter. They used to laugh together, the same way he and Amy laughed. Over silly things that only they understood. And they kissed, not bothering to hide their affection in front of him and his brothers.

He'd never thought about the relationship between the two of them until now. But there must have been a passion there, something that held them together during the long absences. His mum had never talked about it, but then he'd never asked. He and his siblings had always been reluctant to say anything, knowing that she was still mourning her husband twenty years later.

But that was exactly why this thing he had with Amy couldn't last beyond this trip. One wrong step on a mountainside somewhere and she'd be a grieving widow and single parent, just like his mother. He looked down into Amy's eyes and smiled. No, they couldn't have this for long, but Mal was determined to enjoy it while it lasted.

Bending close, he covered her lips with his, the familiar taste of her mouth acting like a drug on his senses. This addiction was getting out of control, a habit he needed to feed every few hours. Touch, taste, a long look or the sound of her voice. It didn't matter what it was.

Her fingers fumbled with the zipper on his jacket and when she finally got it down, she pushed the down-filled fabric aside and pulled his warm body against hers. As they snogged in the snow, they struggled to find familiar spots, skin-to-skin contact to satisfy the desires burning inside them both.

The sky was cloudless and there was no wind, but the winter sun hung lower on the horizon, offering little in the way of warmth. But it didn't matter. The cold couldn't penetrate the haze of passion that enveloped them.

He yanked her jacket aside, then made his way through the layers until he found the soft flesh of her breast. Exposing it briefly to the cold, Mal tongued her nipple until it rose into a stiff peak.

His breath clouded in front of his face as he blew on her nipple, and Amy looked down and smiled. When he moved to the other breast, she moaned softly, furrowing her fingers through his hair.

Mal imagined her naked, the way she'd been last night, her body ripe and ready for his caress. He wanted that now, but it was impossible in the cold and snow. Instead, he slipped his hand beneath the waistband of her pants.

A gasp slipped from her throat when he found the spot. He knew how to make her come quickly. And he knew how to make it last, tormenting her with one slow climb after another. This time around it would be short and sweet, as he didn't want her to get too cold. He'd take the long route later tonight, in the relative warmth of their tent.

Amy closed her eyes as he brought her to the edge, her body responding to his touch as it always did. And when the first wave hit her, she arched her back and grabbed his arm, dissolving into a series of deep spasms. He caught her lips in a long, deep kiss, silencing her moans of pleasure. And when she finally grew still, Mal drew back.

"Now, see? That wasn't a disaster," he teased.

"No," Amy replied, breathless, her face flushed.

"Maybe I'll have to keep you in a constant state of anticipation, just to keep your mind focused and your fears at bay."

"Yes, please," Amy said.

"Do you want to tell me what was bothering you earlier?" he asked.

She shook her head. "Not now."

Mal nuzzled her neck. "You know, if we were in the Himalayas, we wouldn't be able to do this. The Sherpas believe it's disrespectful to engage in carnal activities in such a holy spot. They say it brings bad karma."

"We don't need any bad karma on this trip," she said.

"That doesn't apply to New Zealand mountains," Mal assured her. "Kiwis are a randy lot. We'll shag whenever we come across a pleasant spot on the trail."

"I guess we won't be making any trips to the Himalayas, then."

"I guess not," Mal murmured.

They both knew that Everest was in the Himalayas. She hadn't mentioned the story about his father again. Mal wondered if she'd finally given up, or if she was just gathering her resolve for another attempt.

He knew how much the story meant to her. And if it had only been up to him, he would have assented shortly after she asked. But convincing his two brothers, his sister and his mother was a monumental task, probably more difficult and dangerous than climbing Everest. And he wouldn't put them through that pain.

She'd just have to satisfy herself with this story, the story of a woman who conquered some of her deepest fears on a small mountain in New Zealand.

AMY STARED AT the small notebook she'd brought along to record her thoughts. Throughout the day of training, she'd snapped pictures and jotted down ideas, always searching for a good angle for her story. But try as she might, "Virgin Mountaineer Walks up a Mountain" wasn't nearly as interesting as the story she'd come to New Zealand to tell.

They hadn't talked about his father's story since the day before yesterday. And as much as she was enjoying the trip he was giving her, even the best copy editor, which she was, wouldn't be able to polish it into a diamond. Maybe she just didn't have the distance to tell the story well, since she was both the subject and the reporter.

Or maybe her father was right. Maybe she didn't

have the killer instinct of an adventure writer. There had been moments on the trip as they'd been in the midst of a passionate encounter, when she knew she'd choose sex with Mal over professional success every day and twice on Sunday. But then she'd come back down to earth and realize that in a few days she'd be returning to the real world and her professional goals would be all she had left.

But so far she she'd come up woefully short in achieving those goals. Though she'd considered broaching the subject of the story about Max with Mal again, his trust was still a fragile thing. So Amy decided to focus on the story she actually had in hand and not the one she hoped to have.

"What are you doing?" Mal asked.

He'd been curled up on the other side of the tent, using a small flashlight to read a book he'd brought along. They'd had an early dinner and were due to leave at sunrise the next day to climb to the summit of Mount French. There was an unspoken understanding that they would not be spending the entire night engaged in toe-curling sex.

"I'm just writing a few notes for my article."

"What sort of notes?"

"Just my thoughts about the day. What I learned, things I saw. I'm trying to get my descriptions down while they're vivid in my mind."

"I wonder if that's why my father kept a journal, too. He kept it in his climbing suit. I'm sure he had one the day he died on Everest."

She held her breath, as she always did when he started talking about his father. "Aren't you curious about what he wrote? Maybe he left a message for you and your family," Amy said.

"It's more likely that he wrote details about his final climb. I think that's why Roger Innis is so keen to visit my father's body. He wants to retrieve that notebook before someone else does."

"But wouldn't that be your property? Max was your father."

"I'm sure Roger would claim the journal was a business asset. He's afraid that my father might have written something about the expedition that might reflect badly on him."

"Like what?"

"Like the real reason my dad was on that mountain that late in the day. There have always been rumors that Roger left a client stranded up there and that my dad had turned back to get him. The client made it down and he's never talked about the incident to anyone. My dad didn't return and he *can't* talk to anyone—except through something he might have written in his journal."

"That might be a good reason for you to go and get the journal," Amy suggested.

Mal shook his head. "I just don't think I'm strong enough to do that. I mean, it takes a tremendous amount of energy to climb Everest for anyone. But the emotional energy that it would take me, seeing my father again… I'm not sure I could do it."

Amy's heart ached at the pain she saw in his eyes. They'd never talked about Mal's own reasons for not wanting to make the climb. It had always been about his family's objections. But it was clear he wasn't emotionally prepared to deal with the consequences of seeing his father's lifeless body.

Mal was still facing the repercussions of the tragedy in his everyday life, trying to put it behind him. And with the article, she'd be forcing him to put it front and center, in his head, for at least the next year. "I understand," Amy said. And for the first time, she realized that convincing him might truly be impossible. Without his support, she'd never get anyone else in the family to consent. And in that moment, she felt all her dreams fade to black. There would be no story and no expedition, at least not for the Quinn brothers.

But she wasn't going to let Roger Innis win, either. Mal had expressed an interest in a biography of her father. Maybe *High Adventure* could sponsor a few climbers to retrieve the journal and that would become part of the biography.

Amy turned back to her journal. An uneasy silence fell over the tent. She sensed he wanted to continue talking, but he wasn't sure what he had to say. She started with, "I've seen photos of your father. You look a lot like him."

"Yeah? My mom always used to tell me that when I was a kid. I actually think the twins resemble him more than I do."

"All your memories are so happy. Even though it ended in tragedy."

"My mother would never tell us when he was coming home until the day before he was set to arrive. We'd be so excited, we'd be bouncing off the walls deciding what we wanted to say to him or show him. As an adult, I understand why she did it that way, but as a kid,

I thought she was trying to keep a secret from us and it made me mad."

"Have you told her that?"

Mal shook his head. "We never speak about my dad with her. I mean, he's mentioned in passing, but we don't talk about him. After he died, my mother couldn't even say his name without crying, so we all just stopped bringing him up so she wouldn't get upset. My brothers and I talk about him occasionally. But it's strange how memories can change over time. Rogan and Ryan and I mention things that happened back then, but we're not sure if they're real memories or something we made up in our heads."

"Like what?"

"Like the pony," he said. "Gosh, I haven't thought about that pony in yonks."

"Yonks?" Though it was taking a while, she was learning to understand almost everything he said. *Yonks* was either something the pony wore or a measure of time.

"Yeah. It arrived at our house for the twins' birthday. They were five or six, I think. Or maybe it wasn't for their birthday, but just happened around their birthday. Anyway, we had it for a while, a few days or weeks. And then suddenly it was gone. And I remember my parents fighting about it. Rogan remembers that my dad sent it to them from South America, but how do you send a pony to New Zealand? Ryan said we were just feeding it for a neighbor who had moved and they came and got it later." Mal sighed. "I wish I could ask my mum about it, but I'm always afraid that talking about the past will upset her."

"What does she think about the latest news?"

"I don't know," Mal said with a laugh. "The last time I went to see her, I tried talking to her about it, but I couldn't."

Amy was stunned. This was big news, finding his father's body. And they hadn't even discussed the subject with their mother? "There might not be a better time."

Mal shrugged. "Maxwell Quinn is a mythic figure in our family. If we start discussing what he was really like, I'm afraid of what I might feel if I find out he was just an ordinary man."

He set down the book, then slid across the tent and curled up next to her, resting his head on her lap. Amy closed her pencil inside her journal and smoothed his hair away from his face. "There's nothing wrong with being ordinary," she said.

"You're right," Mal replied. "Maybe I should try to live an ordinary life." He sighed and rolled over onto his back, staring up at her. "I like that we can talk about this."

"Me, too," she said.

"We can always discuss your family," he said.

"Sure. Although that story is just trashy, not tragic. Affairs, mistresses, divorce, child-custody fights. It's like one giant soap opera with a little bit of mountain climbing thrown in."

"Well, if you ever want to open up about it, you can come to me."

Amy bent down and kissed his beard-roughened cheek. "Thanks, I will."

She picked up her journal again and began to scan

the notes while Mal toyed with the fingers of her left hand, weaving them in and out of his.

She had a sudden idea. Maybe the story wasn't about the body on Everest. Maybe her story was about how the ghost of Maxwell Quinn was still haunting his family nearly twenty years later.

Would Mal allow her to tell that story? She'd need to interview his brothers and sister, as well. And his mother. Amy couldn't help but believe that all the silence in their family had been unhealthy for them.

She'd have to do a little more research on that before she brought it up to Mal. The trouble was, she was running out of time. Two weeks might be long enough to enjoy a passionate affair, but it wasn't nearly enough to delve into the psyches of a family of five.

Her instincts said it would be a great story. But she wasn't sure how Mal would react. He might never speak to her again. Was she prepared to sacrifice what she'd found with him for the sake of a story?

They chatted for a little longer about the day ahead of them, then curled up in their sleeping bag and slowly undressed each other until they were naked beneath.

Though Mal had insisted they ought to get to sleep early, neither of them was interested in sleep. Their lovemaking was slow and sweet and filled with unspoken emotion.

Amy knew with every day that passed that it would be painfully difficult to leave Mal. Even without their differing opinions on the story, he wanted nothing more than a temporary affair. And though she found Mal Quinn endlessly attractive, she understood that, though it might be easy for her to fall in love with him, it might be impossible to convince him that he could fall in love with her.

Life on the mountain was simple. Life in the real world was anything but.

6

MAL NEVER SLEPT well before a summit attempt. But with Amy curled up beside him, her warm body wrapped in his arms, he'd been out for at least seven hours.

His internal clock woke him at six and he glanced at his watch, squinting to read the luminescent dial. Six thirty-five. The sun would be up before long and they'd need to leave as soon as they could see the ground in front of them.

He turned on his torch and curled up behind Amy, pressing his lips to her shoulder. "Amy?" he whispered. "Amy, wake up."

"I'm awake," she said.

"I'm going to make breakfast. Then we'll pack up and go."

"I'm not sure I want to eat," she said.

"You have to eat. If you don't, you're going to hit a wall somewhere on the ascent and you won't make it to the top."

"I can't eat," she said. "I'm going to be sick." She groaned softly, then tried to sit up. Suddenly, she crawled across the tent and unzipped the flap, throwing herself out into the cold. He heard her retch and Mal grabbed a bottle of water and held it out to her as she came inside again.

Her teeth were chattering and her body shook. "Come on, get back into the sleeping bag."

"I'm not sure I'm done yet," Amy said, though she complied.

Mal dug through the side pocket in his pack and pulled out a plastic bag. "Here," he said. "Use this. And take a sip of water. It's really easy to get dehydrated if you've got the flu."

"I hate throwing up," Amy said. She pulled the sleeping bag over her head. "Just let me sleep a little longer and I'll be fine."

"No, we're going to stay here until you're feeling better. And then we'll walk down. We have plenty of food, and the weather is holding."

"A little more rest," Amy said, "and I'll be all right."

"We have to leave for the summit now or we won't get up and down the mountain before dark," he said. "And you're in no shape to do anything today. We'll see how you feel tomorrow."

"Yes," she murmured. "I'll be better tomorrow."

She slept for the rest of the morning and Mal left her alone, checking in every now and then with water and a little something to eat. Amy refused the food and could only manage a few sips of water at a time. He worried that it might be more than the flu, that she had some undiagnosed illness.

They weren't high enough for altitude sickness or edema. She didn't have a headache and she wasn't losing her vision or slurring her speech. Hell, he shouldn't be surprised that she was sick. They'd been operating on very little sleep, and just five days ago, she'd flown halfway around the world. And he'd worked her hard yesterday, trying to fit in a two-day mountaineering course into eight hours.

Maybe he'd been too hard on her. It was difficult to view her as just another client, through an objective lens. He wanted her to get the most out of the trip, and purely for his own selfish reasons—so that the article she'd write might appear in *High Adventure*. He wanted Maximum Adrenaline to be known as a tough, aggressive company, not guys who babied their clients while they dragged them up the mountainside with their espresso machines and laptop computers.

Instead he'd made Amy sick. Mal was well aware how serious an illness could be, especially when they were stuck in such a remote location. If things took a turn for the worse, he'd be forced to hike down to the French Ridge hut and use the Department of Conservation radio to call for help. Or he could force her to walk off the mountain right now, before he had to carry her off.

He crawled back into the tent at noon to check on her. She was awake, reading the novel that he'd brought along. "I was thinking we ought to pack up and tramp down. If you get sicker, at least help will be close by."

"I'm feeling much better now," Amy said. "I'll be fine tomorrow. We can hike to the summit then."

"Are you sure?"

Amy nodded. "Yes. I'm sure it's just one of those twenty-four-hour bugs."

"Is there anything you need?" he asked.

"A real bathroom would be nice," she murmured.

"Anything else?"

"Could you rub my feet? My mom always used to do that when I was sick."

"I might be able to manage that," Mal said.

He unzipped the sleeping bag and she stuck out her left foot. Mal pulled off his gloves and began to gently knead the bones and muscles. He brought her foot up to his lips and pressed a kiss into the arch.

"You never talk much about your parents," he said. "Especially your father."

"I didn't see much of him. I didn't really spend time with him at all."

"Kind of like my father," he murmured.

"No, not like your father. You loved your father, I hated mine."

He was shocked by the bitterness in her voice. Amy had never displayed any degree of hostility and he'd assumed it wasn't part of her personality. Mal could only write off her sudden venom as a side effect of her illness. "Why is that?"

"For my sixteenth birthday, I convinced him to take me on an adventure with him. I was so excited to be going on a trip with him. He was going to take me rock climbing. He sent me all the clothes and we flew to California on his jet. And I thought if I could prove to him that I was as brave as my brother, maybe he'd take me along more often."

Mal didn't like where the story was going and he felt his anger begin a slow burn. Richard Engalls had a reputation of being an impatient prick with his guides and support staff. Had he been any different with his own daughter?

"We went out the next day and I was so nervous, I threw up twice, but I was determined to show him that I could do whatever he asked of me. At first, it was going well and I was doing a decent job of climbing. And then I looked down and freaked out. I mean really freaked out, crying and screaming I was so terrified. He could have brought me down, but he refused. He made me climb all the way to the top. It took me three hours to complete a ten-minute climb. After that, I wouldn't speak to him. He sent me back to my mother on the corporate jet. Alone. And ever since, no matter what I do, he assumes I'm going to fail."

"And that's why you got upset yesterday," Mal said. "Because I was pushing you like your father did. And that's why you're sick today."

"No," she said, shaking her head. But then she considered his statement for a long moment and shrugged. "Maybe. I really thought I'd come to terms with that day, but perhaps that is where my fears were coming from. I wasn't really afraid of crevasses and avalanches. I was afraid of failing."

"If that's how you feel about your father, how can you work for him?" Mal asked. "Why not just find a job at another magazine?"

"He used to always tell me that I was my mother's daughter. David was his son, but I took after my mother. Whenever we were together, he'd say horrible things about her and I'd be forced to listen. My father does not tolerate mistakes in his life and she was his biggest—and only—mistake."

"But he's the one who had all the affairs," Mal said.

"And they were her fault. If she'd been the right kind of wife, he wouldn't have strayed, blah, blah, blah. She was the one who insisted on the divorce. She was so unhappy."

"I still don't understand why you stay. You're smart and talented."

"I guess I just want to prove to him that he can't judge me based on what happened between him and my mother. I'm not her."

He reached out and took her hand, pressing a kiss to her fingertips. "Amy, this story you want to do about my father, is it just a way to get your father's attention?"

She pushed up on her elbows and looked down at him, her hair tumbling around her pale face. "No!" A frown wrinkled her brow as she considered the notion. "No! It would be a good story. It's something I want to write."

"But it might get you promoted at your father's magazine."

"Yes, maybe. But that's not the only reason." She buried her face in her hands and groaned. "Do you really believe that's what I'm doing?" She sighed and flopped back down. "Maybe you're right."

Mal slid up to lie at her side, her gaze searching his face.

"I convinced myself that this was all to impress my boss, that this trip was all about my professional goals. But maybe I still want my father to be proud of me, to prove to him that I can do it."

"And I'm dragging you through all this to make it

happen," Mal muttered. "Just like he forced you up the rock."

Amy reached out and took his hand, hooking her finger around his. "I wanted to come," she said.

"Why?"

"To prove it to myself. And maybe to give me more chances to finally convince you to do the story," she admitted.

"You didn't want to come just because we have fun together?"

"Of course. I mean, that was part of the reason. And I hoped I might be able to come away with at least some kind of article, so my trip wouldn't be a total failure."

"And where do we—you and me—fall on the scale of success and failure? Because in my mind, this trip has been more about us than any stupid article."

"I—I don't know." She pressed her hand to her forehead. "I'm still sick and you're giving me a headache. And my fever might be back."

Mal leaned over her and pressed a kiss to her forehead. Her smooth skin was cool. "I think you're on the mend now. Do you want to try to eat something?"

"Maybe," Amy said. "Soup would be good. A little of that chicken noodle."

"I'll make you some," Mal said.

He leaned in to brush a kiss across her lips but she covered her lips with her hand. "Don't. You'll catch what I have."

Mal gently drew her fingers away and kissed her. "We've been swapping spit for days now. If I'm going to get sick, we wouldn't be able to stop it now."

"I don't want to wreck your trip, too."

"You'd never do that, Amy. It doesn't matter what we're doing. I like spending time with you. Even when you're chundering."

She shuddered. "I hate being sick."

"I could always walk out and get you some ginger beer. That's what my mother always gave us when we were sick."

"Would you walk out and get us a pizza?" Amy asked.

"Are you hungry for pizza?"

"No, I was just wondering how much further you'd go to make me feel better."

He picked up her hand and kissed her wrist. "Sweetheart, I'll do whatever it takes to make you smile."

As they continued to chat, Mal thought about those words. There was a simple truth to the statement, and with it came a deeper realization. He would do anything to make her happy. Mal had come to live for her smile and her laugh, those tiny moments that they shared. They'd become as important to him as breathing.

Hé wondering what it would be like in a few days when that was all gone, when she'd left him to return home. Would his life seem suddenly empty, or would some other fascination come along to occupy his thoughts?

Though there was no way to avoid the future, Mal wanted to stay in the present just a little longer.

SHE'D DREAMED OF her father the night before her climb, about that day on the rock. She kept climbing, but no matter how hard she worked, she couldn't get to the top. The sheer face grew beneath her until she was so high off the ground she couldn't see anything below.

It was a terrible dream, one she'd never had before. And when she awoke, Amy wondered if it foretold failure that day. She'd had a restless night, her stomach still giving her problems, but as the sun came up, Amy decided that if she could walk, she was going to walk up that mountain.

She wasn't afraid, and she didn't need to prove anything to anyone—except herself. She was in competent hands; she trusted Mal more than she'd ever trusted any man before.

They climbed all morning and when they finally reached the summit, Amy stood looking out at the stunning vistas and she realized why Mal did what he did. There was a deep satisfaction in being able to push your fears aside and conquer a tiny piece of the planet.

In one direction was Mount Aspiring, the peak that the park had been named for. And a quarter turn revealed Mount Avalanche. The craggy, snow-covered peaks stabbed into the clear blue sky with such power that it took her breath away.

"It's beautiful," she said, glancing over at Mal.

"It never gets old," he said.

The trip to the summit had been long and, at times, difficult for Amy. But Mal had been patient and encouraging, understanding that she was still suffering the aftereffects of the upset she'd battled the day before.

He'd almost refused to take her up the mountain, but when she ate a huge breakfast and guzzled down a full bottle of water, he finally relented. He did make her promise that if she experienced any residual symptoms she had to tell him immediately and they'd start back down.

They'd crossed the glacier at a good pace and dropped their packs on the spot he called the Quarterdeck. From then on, the climb became much easier. Amy felt as if she'd suddenly regained her full strength and balance, and with the adrenaline coursing through her body she scampered up the ridge like a cat.

Mal led the way with Amy roped into his harness about thirty feet behind him. But there were times when she'd almost caught up with him and he'd scold her and remind her to conserve her energy. And then they'd reached the top.

"We should take a few pictures," Mal said. "Just to prove you were really here."

"And this isn't some photographer's backdrop?"

"Give me your camera."

Amy lifted the strap over her neck and handed it to him. He snapped a few photos from different angles, then joined her on the slab of rock and took a few of them together, with Mount Aspiring in the background.

"Now you," Amy said. "I want some only of you."

"Not for the article," he said. "This isn't about me. You're the client."

"No, these are just for me," she said. "For after I go home. To remember you."

He climbed up on the rock. "In that case, let me give you a good shot." He quickly stripped out of his jacket and fleece, then pulled his shirt over his head. When his chest was bare, Mal flexed his biceps and smiled. "How's that?" he called.

"Perfect," Amy said.

She took a few pictures, both a front and back view, then slipped the camera around her neck again.

"You want me to take my pants off?" Mal asked.

"No! Put your clothes on."

"It would make a really great picture. For your personal album, that is."

"I'm sure my imagination will suffice," she said. "You're going to freeze to death. Come on down."

He quickly dressed and climbed down, pulling her into his arms the moment he reached her. "Time to go down. The sooner we get to the hut, the sooner I can rip all your clothes off and have my way with you."

"Can't we stay a little longer?" she asked.

"Nope. Remember, we talked about turnaround time? Remind me what I said."

Amy had listened to his lecture twice. Turnaround time was the point in the day where the trip down had to begin. It was carefully calculated to give the climber the best chance of descending safely while there was plenty of daylight left.

"We never go past our turnaround time," she said. "Never, ever."

It was actually a fitting metaphor for their relationship, Amy mused. How many more days could she spend with Mal before it became impossible to leave him, before walking away would cause her unbearable heartache? Was she already past the point of no return? Or could she still save herself?

Amy glanced over at him and her breath caught in her throat. The idea of never looking into those beautiful blue eyes again, never being able to kiss that crooked smile or touch that perfect body, made her ache inside.

Yes, she was well past her turnaround time. In fact, she'd already tumbled down the mountain and was lying at the bottom, dazed and confused. But this tramp up the peak had proved one thing—she was stronger than she'd ever believed. She'd survive Mal Quinn with the same determination that had brought her to the summit.

Amy threw her arms around his neck and kissed his cheek, her climbing helmet bumping against his. "Thank you for bringing me here. Today has been the best day of my life."

Every day with Mal seemed to be better than the next, in fact. What would it be like to live with him, to know that they had an endless string of days and weeks ahead of them just waiting to be enjoyed? What if she didn't turn around at all, but just stayed here?

It wouldn't be all adventure all of the time. There would be quiet moments together, dinners on the porch and breakfasts in bed. And there would be days and weeks when she'd be alone, waiting for him to come home from another trip. Though it would be difficult to live without him, the certainty that he'd be back in her life someday was much better than wondering if he'd found passion with another woman.

She pressed her palm to her chest and took a quick breath, trying to rid herself of the ache inside and remember to be practical. She ought to be grateful for the time they'd had and not imagine that they could be something more than just temporary lovers. Wanting more than he was willing to give would only cause heartbreak in the end.

Mal walked up to her and held out an energy bar and

his bottle of water. "Here," he said. "You'll need some carbs for the trip down."

Amy took off her helmet and sat down in the snow. Mal plopped down beside her. She opened the wrapper with her teeth and shoved the scraps of plastic in her pocket. As she munched on the granola and chocolate, he reached over and straightened her hat, tugging it down over her ears.

She smiled to herself. It was one of those little gestures that told her he always put her safety and comfort first. That he watched out for her. She felt safe with him, assured that he was always one step ahead of whatever danger was lurking around the next bend.

"I like that hat on you," he said.

He'd chosen an alpaca hat, with a pretty design knit into it and flaps that covered her ears. Decorative ties dangled from the flaps. Amy looked up at him and grinned. "I like it, too. I think I look particularly fetching in it, don't you? It's much prettier than that helmet."

He reached out and pushed the hat down over her eyes in a playful gesture. "You're always fetching. More so when you're not wearing clothes, though, than when you're bundled up in three layers."

She finished the energy bar and took a long drink of water, then handed him the bottle to put back in his jacket.

"Ready?" he asked.

Amy nodded. "Can I lead?"

"I'm not sure about that...."

"I'll follow the tracks that we made coming up. I can do it. I want to do it." It was another challenge, another way to prove to herself that she wasn't afraid. She'd wasted so much of her life dwelling on her doubts and insecurities. And now that she felt herself rising above them, Amy wanted to see just how far she could push herself.

Mal considered her request for a second then nodded. "Just remember what I taught you. Every footstep counts. Make sure your footing is sound before you shift your weight. And use your poles for balance, even if you think you don't need them. Better to be safe than sorry."

"All right." She checked the clip on her harness and grabbed the rope in her gloved hand. She stood and took in the incredible view of the surrounding mountains for one last moment then turned to him. "Ready?"

"Lead on," Mal said.

Amy stared down the ridge, her gaze following the footsteps that had brought them up to the summit. For the first time in her life on this ledge, she'd felt as if she could conquer anything.

Sure, it was a small peak. But it had been her emotional Everest, a chance to prove to herself that she could do anything she set her mind to.

She was coming down a different person than she'd been on the way up.

To MAL'S SURPRISE, Amy was quite confident in the lead. He watched her carefully from the rear and was impressed that she painstakingly followed his instructions. In truth, she had more presence of mind on the trip down that many professional climbers he'd seen. She was careful in every footstep, placing her poles first before moving.

Whether it came naturally or out of a fear of tumbling down the mountainside, he wasn't sure. But Mal wanted to believe that it was because he was a good teacher. He had to give himself credit for achieving that in his life. He might not have scaled Everest three times before his thirtieth birthday. Nor had his climbing abilities garnered worldwide fame. His business was still struggling. But he knew how to guide and to teach, and he was proud of that.

His gaze dropped to Amy's bum and his mind wandered to what they would do once they arrived at the hut. Hopefully, they'd be alone, and if they weren't, they pitch their tent outside. He'd strip off her bulky climbing pants and the fleece and then he'd—

Mal heard the snap of bone before he even realized what had happened. The rock beneath his foot gave way and he tried to catch himself, but then he was down and it was over.

The pain came a few seconds later and he lay back and fought a wave of nausea. He was almost afraid to look, knowing his limb would be good and broken. That sound was something you didn't forget, and he'd heard it before—once as a kid when he'd jumped out of a tree and another time when he'd fallen off his mountain bike.

A flood of curse words slipped from his lips as he rolled to his side. Shit. He'd made a stupid mistake and he'd put them both at risk. He should have been watching his step rather than indulging in fantasies of what he and Amy would do once they reached the shelter. He'd been fantasizing about sex and the gods of the glacier had decided to punish him for it.

Amy didn't realize what had happened until the rope went taut. She turned around and looked up at him, and an instant later, began a mad scramble to the spot where he lay.

"Are you all right?" She knelt beside him and scanned his expression. "What happened? Did you fall?"

"I just broke my ankle," Mal said.

She gasped, pressing her hand to her chest. "What?"

"The rock gave way. I slipped and tried to catch myself and it just snapped."

"How can that happen?"

"It does," Mal said. "A lot more often than you think." He groaned. "Shit! Goddammit, it hurts."

"What are we going to do? Can you walk?"

"No, I don't think so. Not without leaning on you, and that would put us both in danger."

"I have to get help," she said.

Mal shook his head. "No. You'll stay right here and we'll wait. It's the weekend. Someone will be climbing this route. They can get help for us."

He shifted and the pain in his ankle shot all the way up his leg, taking his breath away. "Fuck. Oh, bloody hell, it hurts. This is my fault. Completely my fault. I was just tramping along, staring at your bum and wasn't watching where I was going and—"

"You were staring at my ass? What about all those lessons you gave me about focus and concentration and putting one foot firmly in front of the other?"

"I don't always practice what I preach," he muttered. "Sue me."

"It's my fault," Amy said.

"For what? Having a nice bum?"

"No, for insisting that I take the lead."

"Don't be ridiculous." He glanced at his watch.

"Damn. There's about three hours of daylight left. We're about an hour away from French Ridge Hut. No one is going to be climbing up tonight."

"Then I'll go down and get help. Maybe someone is staying at the hut tonight. You said it wasn't a long hike. I can get there and we can find a way to get you down tonight." She met his gaze with a stubborn resolve. "You taught me everything I need to know. I can do this."

He'd grabbed a satellite phone before he'd left, but realized later that the battery hadn't been recharged. It had been a stupid mistake, but one he'd brushed aside, certain that if something went wrong, he could hike out for help. He just never thought he'd make two stupid mistakes on one trip.

He looked at Amy's determined face. Mal could see how much this meant to her. Over the past few days, she'd gained so much confidence in herself that he believed she was completely able to finish the tramp down to the hut and call for help on the radio.

Still, there were risks. She'd be on her own. A simple slip and fall of her own could put her in exactly the position he was, without a functioning leg. "No," he finally said. "There's just too many things that can go wrong."

"I'm going," she said stubbornly. "We'll set up the tent and get you settled and I'll hike down to the hut. If there's someone there we'll figure how to come back up and get you."

"There's a radio there," he said. "You can call for help. But you have to promise me that you're not going to hike back up here after you call. Even if you think you'll have time. You'll stay in the hut for the night. Promise?"

"I don't like the idea of you being alone, especially when you're injured."

"It's not that cold, Amy, and I've got the tent and food and water. It won't be comfortable, but I'm not going to die on this mountain." He didn't realize until he'd said those words how worried she was. She blinked back tears, then forced a bright smile.

"Of course you're not going to die. Don't be silly."

Was this how it had happened with his father? Some simple mistake that had blown into a terrible tragedy? Maxwell Quinn had been faced with much more dire circumstances—hours from help, no oxygen, bad weather rolling in and temperatures far more extreme than this. This was like a Sunday stroll in the park compared to an overnight near the summit of Everest.

"I'm going to set up the tent," she said. Amy stepped behind him and gently helped him out of his pack. She unclipped his sleeping bag and pulled it out, then wrapped it around his shoulders.

She worked with single-minded efficiency and Mal was surprised at how easily she got the tent up. When she was finished, she hurried back over to him. "All right. I'm going to take the climbing gear out of my pack and leave my extra clothes here. Some of the food, too. If I'm carrying less, I can move faster." She reached inside her jacket and handed him the notebook she'd been using to record her thoughts. "All right, tell me where I'm going."

He pointed off to the right. "Follow the ridge down, the same way we've been going for the past hour. You'll see the hut after about fifteen minutes. It's bright red. You won't be able to miss it."

"Maybe we should make a splint before I leave. Just so you're more comfortable."

Mal took her hand and pressed his lips to her fingertips. "Remember the rule that you had to do whatever I say? Well, this is the reason I have that rule. You need to leave now while you have good light."

"All right," Amy said as she put on her helmet. "Follow the ridge until I see the red hut."

"Right," he replied. "There'll be heat at the hut and a dunny, so you'll be comfortable for the night. Use your poles on the walk down. You cannot fall and hurt yourself. You have to be careful with every single step. Understand?"

She nodded, her eyes suddenly swimming with tears. One trickled out of the corner of her eye and froze on her cheek. Mal reached out and wiped it away. "This is the easy part of the trip. It's all downhill, and you have perfect weather and plenty of light. They'll probably take me straight to the hospital, so you'll have to meet me there. I arranged for one of our guides, Adam Sullivan, to wait for us at the Raspberry Flats car park at five tomorrow evening. He was going to drive us back to Christchurch. Tell the warden and they'll drop you there. Adam will know how to find me."

"All right," she said, brushing away the tears. She bent down and kissed him, her lips soft and sweet against his. "Now, let's get you inside the tent before I leave."

Mal shook his head. The pain would probably be excruciating and he didn't want her to see that. She'd be even more worried and might make a misstep on the descent. "No, I'm going to stay out here and watch you go down." He laughed at a sudden thought. "This is going to add a whole new level of drama to your story. Just promise me you won't write that bit about looking at your bum."

"I promise." She kissed him again. "I'm going to go now. You stay safe."

"I will. I'm going to make a splint from my poles to stabilize my ankle. It's really not that bad." Mal watched as she lifted her pack onto her shoulders. "Be careful."

"I will," she said.

She took her first step away from him and Mal felt an ache in his heart so strong that he couldn't breathe. She'd be fine. He'd watched her gain incredible confidence over the past few days, and the rest of the tramp wasn't that difficult.

This was exactly why a guide shouldn't get involved with a client, Mal chided himself. Until now, he hadn't realized how one simple mistake could cascade into an avalanche of problems. He'd taken one of his cardinal rules lightly and bent it and twisted it to suit his own needs. He'd put pleasure before business and risked both their lives.

Was he crazy to let her go? Even though the hike down was easy, he'd broken his own ankle on the same kind of terrain. What if she fell? Who would be there to help her? "Amy!"

She was already too far away to hear him, though, the wind tossing his words back into his face before they could reach her. Mal closed his eyes and rested his head on the snow, staring up at the clear blue sky.

At least she had good weather. There wasn't a cloud for miles.

He carefully went through all the risks in his head. To Amy and to himself. Though he was pretty sure the ankle was broken, he wasn't sure of the severity of the break. There was always a chance of complications if he went without treatment for too long. And if she'd stayed, it could have been days before anyone else happened by them.

No, he'd been right to send her down. He was no good to her here and he had no idea what tomorrow might bring. She was focused and determined and she'd be safe for the night. Mal winced. And she wouldn't have to see him struggle with the pain. For that, he was grateful.

But then he thought of her article again. His fall would definitely add drama to the story. And it would be horrible for his reputation. With one wrong step, he may have ruined his business.

7

AMY PACED BACK and forth, covering the length of the lobby in the warden's office in seven long steps. She'd spent the night wrapped in her sleeping bag and worried about the man she'd left behind on the mountain.

As he'd promised, the hike to the hut had been easy and she'd made it well before dark. There were three climbers there when she arrived and they'd helped her radio the warden, then got her settled in for the night.

Though she'd hoped that they'd find a way to get Mal down that night, they'd decided to send a pair of rescue climbers up to evacuate him first thing in the morning. Her request to accompany them was firmly denied.

That had been hours ago.

Until this long period of waiting, she'd been a model of calm and efficiency. She'd asked the warden to contact Mal's office and she'd arranged to have Adam meet her earlier than planned. The warden had said that they'd most likely take Mal out by helicopter and he'd either land in Wanaka or, if the medics felt his condition was serious, they'd take him directly to a hospital in Queenstown.

Adam had arrived, and then they'd waited for news. Every minute seemed like an hour. First there was a delay with the helicopter, then they'd been informed that he'd be coming by ambulance instead. After asking for her tenth progress report, she'd decided to try pacing instead.

"I'm surprised he didn't take the satellite phone with him," Adam said. "That's not like him."

Amy stopped pacing. "He has a satellite phone?"

Adam nodded. "Yeah, he takes it on every expedition. It's expensive to make a call, but in an emergency, it's the best way to get help."

"This trip was supposed to be easy," she said. "That's what he kept saying. And it was, until he broke his leg."

"He's a tough bloke," Adam said. "It's going to take a lot more than a bad ankle to keep him down."

"How long have you known him?" Amy asked, plopping down in the chair next to Adam.

"Long time. We climbed together when we were teenagers. I did one of my first climbs in the Southern Alps with Mal when we were seventeen. He drove all the way down from Raglan in this beat-up Toyota. He'd told his mother he was going fishing. Crikey, the lies we used to come up with to make climbing trips. When he finally decided to leave the country to climb, he was forced to own up to her. She was not chuffed, let me say."

Amy smiled. "He has a way of getting what he wants when he wants it, though."

"Very true."

The door to the offices opened and a woman poked her head out. "Mrs. Quinn?"

Amy glanced around the room and Adam gave her a jab with his elbow. "Yes?" she said.

"Your husband will be here in Wanaka in a few minutes. They brought him out by ambulance. He's going to the medical center where they'll evaluate his injuries. You can meet him there."

Amy jumped up and turned to Adam. "Do you know where that is?"

"Take a right from the car lot," the woman instructed, "and then your next left, just past the park. Follow Mc-Dougall Street through town until it turns to Cardona Valley Road. It's not a long drive."

They hurried out to Adam's car and fifteen minutes later pulled into the clinic car park. Adam dropped her off at the front door and told her he'd wait for her in the lobby if she needed any help.

Amy ran inside and stopped at the reception desk. "I'm here to see Malcolm Quinn. He's been brought in with a broken ankle?"

"Yes," the woman said. "He's just arrived. And you are?"

"I'm Amy—" She paused. "I'm his wife, Amy Quinn." Apparently it wasn't enough to be Mal's lover or client. The only way she'd gotten information at the warden's office was because Adam had told them she was Mal's wife. Maybe that would work here, too.

"I'll just get a nurse to take you back," the woman said, reaching for the phone.

Amy took a seat and waited. Adam joined her a few minutes later. "How is he?"

"He just got here," she said. "I'm Mrs. Quinn again, by the way."

Adam chuckled. "Congratulations," he said. "I hope you'll be very happy together. Any plans for a family?"

Amy slapped his arm. "No. And, as a point of etiquette, you say 'best wishes' to the bride and 'congratulations' to the groom."

"I'll remember that when I have to do it for real," he said.

Amy blinked. "Oh, we're not... Mal and I are just... There's nothing serious between us. I'm just a client."

"Really? It didn't seem that way when he was telling me about this trip." He shrugged. "He usually doesn't talk so much about clients."

"Mrs. Quinn? You can come with me."

Amy turned and gave Adam a grateful smile. "I'll give you an update when I have one." She hurried after the nurse who led her through a series of exam rooms. She motioned Amy through an open door. Mal was lying on an examining table, his leg encased in a huge splint. His eyes were closed and at first she thought he was sleeping.

"Mal?"

He sat up, bracing himself with his elbows. "Hey, there. Congrats, I knew you could do it."

She crossed the room and threw her arms around him. "I was so worried about you. I was afraid something was wrong when it took so many hours." She cupped his face in her hands and kissed him. "Are you okay? Does it hurt?"

"No. Kisses make it much better."

She rained kisses all over his face. "Watch out," he

said. "I've got a wife wandering around here some-where. I don't want her to catch us snogging."

"I had to give them the lie about being your wife," she said. "They wouldn't tell me anything if I wasn't."

"Does this mean I only get sex on birthdays and an-niversaries?"

She slipped his arm around her waist and leaned over him. "You must be fine if you're talking about sex."

"It would take a lot more than a broken ankle to stop me." His hand drifted down to her backside and he gave her a squeeze. "Now give me another kiss, and make it a good one."

Amy leaned in, but, just as she expected, the doc-tor strode through the door a second later, clipboard in hand.

"Malcolm Quinn? I'm Doctor Kessel." The doctor held out his hand and Mal shook it.

"Mal," he replied.

"Yes. I've read about you. I did one of your moun-taineering courses a couple years ago. You weren't the teacher, but we enjoyed a lot of stories about the ex-ploits of you and your brothers." He turned to Amy. "Mrs. Quinn?"

"Amy," she said, shaking his hand.

He pulled an X-ray out of an envelope and clipped it onto a lighted panel. "So what happened here?" Dr. Kessel asked as he studied the film.

"Simple slip and fall," Mal said. "The rock crumbled under my foot and I tried to catch myself and my foot landed wrong."

"Well, you've broken both the bones right above the ankle. It's a fairly common injury for a slip and fall.

You have two choices. We can set it and put a cast on. That'll take at least three months to heal. Or we can do surgery and stabilize it with a plate and screws. You'll be up and walking again in about six weeks. I assume you'll want to do the latter."

"You assume right," Mal said. "I can't afford to be out of work for three months."

"You'll still have to take it easy. I suspect you may have torn some of the ligaments, as well. Your ankle may never be as strong as it once was. But with therapy, you'll be able to walk without a problem."

"What about climbing?"

"Well," the doctor said, "I'll be honest with you. Some people never regain a full range of motion. But we can remove the plate and screws once the bone is healed, and hopefully that will help. In about half the cases I treat, the ankle is permanently weakened. We'll just have to see how it goes."

Amy took a deep breath and forced a smile, giving Mal's hand a squeeze. She'd never thought that his injury might permanently prevent him from doing what he loved.

She fought back a wave of guilt. Two people involved in a sexual affair should not be climbing together. The Sherpas on Everest had the right idea. It was bad karma. And bad sense. There were just too many distractions that could easily end in injury—or death.

Still, Amy was grateful that even if Mal's career might be over, he'd come out of it alive. He was here, in one piece, breathing and laughing and kidding with her.

But all joking had been put aside for the moment

with the doctor. "Then I'm just going to have to do everything I can to get it strong again."

"Good," Dr. Kessel said. "That's the attitude you'll need. Now I'm going to put some paperwork together and we're going to send you to Queenstown for the surgery. They'll be able to do it tomorrow if the swelling goes down enough. You'll be able to fly back home as soon as they release you."

"Thanks," Mal said. "And as soon as you want to do another climb, call the office and I'll arrange it. No charge. Wait until I'm on my feet again, though, and I'll take you myself."

"I'll do that," the doctor said.

When they were alone, Amy kissed Mal again. He groaned softly and she drew back. "Does it hurt?"

"It's mostly my pride now. I can't believe I did something so incredibly stupid."

"Didn't they give you pain medication?"

"Yeah, but I like your medicine better. I think I might need something stronger than a kiss, though."

"Like what?" Amy asked.

"Maybe you could open up your shirt? That will make me feel even better."

Amy gasped. "You perv! That pain medication is making you loopy."

"Not loopy," he said. "Horny. Now come on, show me a little skin. I promise I won't touch, I'll just look."

Amy glanced around the room, then turned her back to the door and quickly flashed him. "Satisfied?"

"No, but it will have to do for now," Mal said, his lips curled into a wicked grin.

For now. That was all she could focus on, too.

MAL HAD TROUBLE sleeping in the hospital in Queenstown. He'd doze off for a few minutes or even an hour, then wake up to some strange sound—a bell or a buzzer or a voice over the PA system. They'd wanted him to take more painkillers, but the drugs made his mind fuzzy.

And his mind was a jumble of crazy thoughts—about Amy, about his injury, about his father. No matter what subject he turned his mind to, all he could see was trouble ahead for him. His injury was the worst of his worries. Right now, he and his brothers divided the work of the business evenly. But with Mal on crutches, they'd have to hire an extra guide for the trips he couldn't lead. That would cut into the profits and make the finances even tighter for the next six months.

If he did the article about his father with Amy, he might be able to mitigate some of the loss. A series of features in *High Adventure* would bring in a lot more business, making it possible to hire more guides. And it would avoid the embarrassment and potential loss of business from his injury being described there instead. But looming over all this was the prospect of facing the past. Was he finally ready to deal with his father's death? And what about Rogan and Ryan? And his mother and Dana? If they fought him on this, he'd never go ahead alone.

And then there was Amy's idea about a biography of Max. Though that kind of project would give his family more control, it wouldn't give them an immediate influx of cash. There had to be a way to work through this that didn't involve tearing his family apart. He just couldn't see it right now.

Mal shifted in bed, rubbing a cramp out of his back. He wasn't used to just lying around.

His broken ankle was encased in a cast and elevated in a sling. He'd been forced to use a bedpan, calling the nurse whenever he had to go. But they'd promised that they'd let him out of bed in the morning to walk on crutches.

He opened his eyes and stared out the window, trying to guess the time of day by the amount of light shining through the blinds. Amy had arrived in Queenstown that afternoon during his surgery and had left a few hours ago to rent a room at a nearby hotel and take a shower. She'd promised to come back before dinner.

A knock sounded on the door and he turned to find his mother walking into the room. "Are you awake?"

Mal pushed up on his elbows. "Mum? What are you doing here?"

"I had to make sure you were all right," she said, her face filled with worry. "When Adam called, Dana and I got on a flight and came down here. He said you had to have surgery."

"It's nothing," Mal said. "A broken ankle. They took me to the clinic in Wanaka first and when they decided I needed surgery, then sent me down here in an ambulance."

"Surgery?"

"They had to stabilize the break with a plate and screws. It'll be good as new in a few months." He held out his hand. "I'm sorry I scared you. I should have called to tell you not to come."

She took his hand and pressed it to her heart as she slowly sat in the chair beside the bed. "I can't go through this again," she murmured. "I can't lose one of you to another mountain or glacier or whatever horror is out there waiting for you."

Mal squeezed her hand. "This was nothing, Mum. I could have done much worse running up the stairs at the office or riding my bike. It was just a stupid mistake. I wasn't watching where I was going and it just happened."

"And why weren't you watching where you were going? You promised me you'd always be careful."

"I was distracted." Mal paused, wondering if he ought to give her the entire story. Maybe it would help soothe some of her fears. "I met this girl. Woman, actually. And I decided to take her out on a bit of an adventure. I was staring at her bum when I put my foot down wrong and that's how it happened."

His mother frowned. "The least you could do is make up a plausible lie. I know you and your brothers keep the truth from me because you're afraid I can't handle it, but I deserve a bit more respect than some silly story about a girl's arse."

Mal was stunned at her suspicions. "It's true," he said. "I've met a woman. She works for a magazine in the U.S. And she's clever and funny and beautiful and—"

"And?"

"And I think I might be falling for her."

"You? In love?"

Mal thought about the question for a long moment. "Yeah. Maybe. I'm not quite sure yet, but it's moving in that direction." He sent her a smile and the anger dissolved from her expression.

"Are you planning to ask this girl to marry you?"

"No," Mal said. "We've only just met. And I've always written off the notion of marriage, assuming it was impossible because of my career and my lifestyle. How did you and Dad make it work?"

"We made it work because we didn't have any choice in the matter. We loved each other."

"And it didn't bother you that he chose to do what he did?"

"Of course it did," she said. "It hurt me and it worried me. I hated it when he left me alone. But it was what he loved to do, it was part of who he was. And I loved him, all of him, top to bottom."

"Why haven't you ever told us this before?" Mal asked. "You never talk about him."

"I guess I don't want to get all weepy in front of you, so I don't bring him up. But there isn't a day, an hour, that goes by that I don't think about him and wish he was here to see how his children have grown."

"And how did you feel when you heard that they'd found his body?"

"Like he'd died all over again. I used to dream, and still do every now and then, that your father would walk in the front door as if he'd just been out for a stroll. He's happy and playful and everything is back to the way it was. In the years right after his death, I used to long for those dreams, wish they'd come true. I'd even make up stories in my head that he'd walked off the mountain the next morning and just got lost, or that he couldn't remember who he was, or he'd been found wandering around by Tibetan monks and they'd kept him in some mountaintop monastery. Any story, as long as it ended with him still being alive."

"We used to do that, too," Mal said. "Me and the twins. We had a lot of fantastic theories about what happened. But as we got older, we just stopped."

"Well, I never did," his mother said. "Not until I heard the news that he'd been found."

"Would you like us to go up there and pay our last respects? We could bring some of his personal effects back for you?"

Lydie Quinn smiled weakly. "A few months ago, I would have said no. Absolutely not. I don't want that mountain taking any more of my family. But now that I've had a chance to think about it, it might be a good idea. You boys need to make peace with what happened before any of you can find true happiness. And if that happens on Everest, then so be it."

"Really?"

"I'm not entirely sure it's a great idea for you to see your father that way. But it's up to you, I won't stop you from going. If you do make the trip, bring his journal home. It's the one volume I'm missing. There's a picture of the two of us that he always kept tucked in the front cover, and I don't have a copy. We took it on our honeymoon and it was always my favorite picture of us together. I know it was his, too. I'd like to have that picture."

"You have his other journals?" Mal asked, shocked.

She nodded. "I'm sorry I told you that I burned them, but I just couldn't face the prospect of hearing you boys read them out loud. Maybe it's time I gave them to you."

"Mum, Amy—the girl I mentioned—she's a writer

for an adventure magazine. She suggested we write a biography about Dad. We could use the journals. It would be a way of making sure that his story is written the way we want it to be written."

"That's a lovely idea," Lydie said. "I want people to know the whole man, not just the man who climbed mountains. When you visit Auckland next, stop by and pick up the journals. I think you'll enjoy them."

She slowly stood, then leaned over to kiss his cheek. "All this talk about your father is exhausting. I'm going to go get a cup of tea. Dana is waiting outside. She'll want to be sure for herself that you're all right."

"Where are you staying?"

"We have a room at an inn not far from here."

"Mum, you can really go home. They're going to let me out tomorrow."

"We'll fly back together," she said.

"My surgeon says I can't fly for a couple of days, so Amy and I are going to hang out here until I can leave. She's stopping by in a bit. I'd like to introduce you."

"Hey, can I come in?"

Dana peeked in the door, then held out a bouquet of flowers in front of her as she walked in. "You're looking much better than I expected," his sister said.

"I'm fine. Just a bloody stupid accident."

"I know. I was talking to Amy out in the lobby," Dana said.

"She's here?"

"Yeah. She figured she'd wait until we'd seen you before she came in."

"This is going to make a very interesting part of her story," Dana said. "How are you going to spin it?"

"Story?" Lydie asked. "What story?"

"Amy came here because she wanted to write a story about us and our father," Dana said.

"She's not doing that story anymore," Mal said. "She's going to write about our trip. And you're the one who said we needed more publicity." He snatched the flowers from her hand. "Why don't you go out and ask her to come in so I can introduce her to Mum."

"Oh, this is serious," Dana said. "You've never introduced a girl to Mum." She turned to Lydie. "He hasn't, has he?"

"I don't believe he has," his mother said.

"That must have been a little more than just a business trip," Dana said in a serious tone.

"If you've come here to torment me, you can take your flowers and leave," Mal said. "Go get Amy."

Dana smiled. "You are fine if you're shouting orders at me like you always do."

When she left the room, he chuckled softly. "Can I ask another question, Mum? Why did you have a fourth child?"

"Because I wanted at least one child who wouldn't want to be hauled up a mountainside by your father." She patted his hand. "You know, Dana is right. You do look good. And happy."

"I am." Though he was happy and still filled with doubts, he was happy.

"IT WAS LOVELY meeting you, Amy. And I hope I have a chance to see you again before you go home to the States."

"I hope so, too," Amy said. "I'm going to fly back to

Auckland with Malcolm. I'll make sure he calls when we arrive."

Dana held out her hand. "Take good care of my big brother," she said.

Amy felt her face flush with warmth. Somehow his mother and sister had gotten the idea that she and Mal were more than just "friends with benefits." They were talking as if she was his girlfriend. In truth, she didn't want them to know the specifics of the arrangement she had with Mal, so in the end, she decided to go along with it, just as she had in the ambulance.

She walked them both to the elevator, then returned to Mal's room. He held out his hand and she crawled into bed with him, snuggling against his body. "Kiss me," she said, angling her face up to his.

Mal pulled her close and gave her a long, lazy kiss, teasing at her tongue with his. "I've wanted to do that since you walked in."

"You look much better than you did after the surgery," she said. "You were kind of goofy with all the painkillers."

"I told them I wasn't going to take the drugs anymore. And I do feel better. I just wish I could get out of bed. I need a shower and a shave."

"When do you get out of the traction?"

"Tomorrow morning. Until then, I'm supposed to use a sponge and a wash basin."

"Maybe I can help," Amy said.

"You're going to give me a bath?"

She sat up and smiled at him. "Sure. It could be fun."

"Oh, naughty nurse!" Mal said, throwing out his arms. "Please, have at it."

Giggling, Amy crawled off the bed and ran to fill the washbasin with warm water. She found a washcloth and towels on the rack, then opened the package that contained the disposable razor.

"I think we'll start with a shave," she said. "You're looking a little scruffy."

The nurse had left a small can of shaving cream, so Amy softened his beard with the washcloth then patted the shaving cream on his face. Leaning over the bed, she drew the razor over his deeply tanned face, rinsing it after each pass.

Mal used the opportunity to run his hand over her backside. When she nicked him with the razor, he stopped his hands from wandering and silently complied with her orders.

They worked out a way to wash his hair, lowering the bed so he could rest his head on the basin while she lathered and rinsed. She liked taking care of him, doing things that made him feel more comfortable. At least she could be of use. She couldn't climb a very tall mountain with him or scale an ice wall, but she could wash his hair.

When they were finished, she rubbed his hair dry with a towel and combed it back from his face. "Much better," she said. "How do you handle this when you're on an expedition?"

"Oh, we wash up," he said. "Just like this. We heat water and have shampoo and soap. But I've never had a beautiful woman to help me out. Now, about the bath…"

"You really want a bath?" she asked.

"Yes, Nurse Amy, I want a bath."

"Then we'd better get you out of that gown."

Amy walked to the door and locked it, and by the time she'd returned to the bed, he'd discarded the gown and was naked. She'd never had a chance to just admire his body, to see it in its complete masculine beauty.

"Are you just going to stand there?" he asked.

"Yes," she said. "I'm allowed to look, aren't I?" Her gaze came to rest on his shaft, already growing hard. "I haven't even touched you."

"It has a mind of its own," Mal said. "I just can't control it. Maybe it would behave itself if you took off some of your clothes."

"No!" Amy cried. "This is supposed to be a bath, not sex."

"Can't it be both?"

"You're going to be doing this all on your own if you don't behave," she warned.

He watched her silently as she ran the soapy sponge over her his chest and shoulders. When she finished that, he raised his hands and she washed his arms. His reaction to the bath was evident.

But she avoided washing his intimate parts, leaving them until the end, knowing that the anticipation would make the task much more fun.

"Are you ready?" she asked.

"Are you not paying attention?" he countered, nodding at his lap.

"I think I'd better get some warmer water. This is a little cold." She walked to the bathroom, and as she filled the basin, she stripped down to her underwear. She'd bought a change of clothes that afternoon and had picked up a pretty pink-and-black bra and matching panties to replace the clean underwear she'd left behind in the tent.

Amy hadn't expected to show them to him until they got back to his cottage in Raglan, but she was sure he'd enjoy them. As she walked out of the bathroom, she turned down the lights in the room to a more romantic glow.

When she moved to the side of the bed, his reaction was exactly as she'd hoped. Grinning, he reached out for her, but she evaded his grasp. "No touching," she said. "Nurse Amy's rule."

It became a long, slow tease and one that they both enjoyed. She took her time soaping his erection, then stroked him, her fingers slick. Mal couldn't move much due to the traction, but Amy used that to her advantage.

He enjoyed the bath, but she wanted to give him more. Amy rinsed off the last of the soap, then continued to caress him. With his leg bent at a clumsy angle, there was no way they could have sex. But she did have options.

Amy pressed her lips to his belly then dropped a trail of kisses to his hip, torturing him a bit longer. When he reached for her, she quickly drew away and wagged her finger at him. "No touching. Bad patient."

Mal chuckled softly. "You're having far too much fun with this. When I get out of this puckaroo, you'll be having a session with Dr. Malcolm. I can promise you that."

"And then *you* can make the rules," she said. "But I'm in charge in this hospital."

"Proceed with your examination," he said, surrendering.

Amy had never felt this free and uninhibited when it came to sex. It had always been such a serious affair with other men. But from the start, she and Mal had taken a different approach, one where there was nothing they couldn't say or do once their clothes came off.

He was teetering on the edge already and when she ran her tongue along the length of his shaft, Mal gasped. Amy took him into her mouth, teasing with her tongue until he was desperate to touch her.

This time, when his fingers tangled in her hair, she didn't stop him. He guided her movements until the moment before he tumbled over the edge. Then he pulled her into a kiss as his body shuddered with pleasure beneath her touch.

When he was finally spent, he growled softly and pressed his lips to her shoulder. "I feel so much better."

"I'm glad I could help," Amy teased.

"Do you think we could find you a little white dress and one of those nurse hats? We need to do this again."

"I was hoping we'd play sexy stable boy next time," Amy said.

"I could do sexy stable boy with a limp," he said.

"That will do," Amy said. She crawled onto the bed with him and he wrapped his arm around her. "Do you think they'd notice if I slept here tonight?"

"We could always try," he said.

Amy closed her eyes. She'd spent a week in his bed and now didn't want to sleep anywhere else. But she had a ticket home dated one week from today. She thought about her flat in Brooklyn, her friends, her job, her big comfy bed. All the things that were so familiar to her.

That was her life. And yet it seemed to be a life that

belonged to somebody else, someone she didn't know. So many things had happened since she'd first set eyes on Malcolm Quinn. She had changed.

But what if she returned to New York and she suddenly transformed back into the quiet, unhappy woman she'd once been? She was tired of always wanting more. Here, with Mal, she had everything she could possibly desire.

If only he wanted it, too.

8

MAL CALLED FOR Duffy and the black Lab ran up to him, the Frisbee in his teeth. As always, the dog was so excited to play that he almost knocked Mal off his crutches.

It was a perfect late-autumn afternoon, the temperatures cool, the air crisp. Mal had been cooped up inside with his broken ankle so much the past couple of days that he was grateful for any opportunity to get out and get some exercise.

"Be careful," Amy shouted from her spot on the porch. "If you break your other ankle you're not going to be able to walk at all."

"Yes, Mother," Mal replied.

Amy sent him a dark look. "You know what you can do with that Frisbee, don't you?"

He chuckled to himself. Though she sounded angry, it was all part of their usual banter. The lighthearted teasing was quite effective in covering the fact that they were both preoccupied with her leaving.

She had a ticket to fly back to the States the day

after tomorrow. The clock had nearly run down on their time together, and they were both coming to grips with the notion that before long, they'd have to live without each other.

Though he wasn't allowed to put any weight on his ankle, that didn't stop him from furiously exercising other parts of his body. He'd decided to do a thousand ab crunches a day, followed by an hour of free weights and one hundred pull-ups. He was still trying to figure out a way to ride his bike using just one foot, and he thought he might be able to manage a rowing machine if he bought one.

Mal threw the Frisbee again, then turned to look at Amy. She was sitting on the rocker, his laptop resting on her thighs. Her own laptop had refused to boot up since she'd dropped it on the pavement the day they'd met.

Duff trotted up to him and Mal hobbled toward the porch. "What are you working on?"

"My story. It's almost done."

"Wow, that was fast."

"No. That's slow. It's taking me forever to get it exactly right."

"Can I read it?" he said, sitting down in the chair beside her.

"Sure." Amy handed him the computer. "If you find any mistakes, just underline them. But you won't find any mistakes." She crawled out of the chair. "I'm going to go start supper. Is spaghetti all right? I found some really good bread at the market this morning."

"You don't have to wait on me," he said. "I'm perfectly capable of doing some of the cooking."

Amy laughed, pulling her sweater more tightly

around her. "Right. Your idea of cooking is calling for takeaway or pouring hot water into a freeze-dried food bag."

"I can work a barbie," he said. "I'm good with meat."

As she walked by him, she ran her hand across his chest. "So am I."

"And you call me a perv," he muttered as she pulled open the front door. He settled back into the rocker, one hand on the computer, the other petting Duff's head.

From the very first line of the story, he was hooked. Amy wrote with such precision and such beauty that he almost didn't believe he'd been on the same trip. She'd noticed things that he'd never given a second look at and turned them into vital pieces of this puzzle she was solving.

The story was about their climb, but it was also a personal story about what she'd learned along the way. And she hadn't mentioned his injury. But the story would never appear on the pages of *High Adventure.* From an adventure standpoint, it wasn't terribly exciting. But as a story of triumph over fear, it was perfect.

When he finished, he leaned back and closed his eyes. She'd never get what she really wanted with this article. And seeing what she'd managed to compose out of such a simple situation, Mal realized that she would do a beautiful job with his family's story.

But was he really willing to expose his mum and siblings to the scrutiny that an article would bring, just so he could make Amy's dreams come true?

And yet even his mother had said they needed to come to terms with the past. And the series that Amy proposed did have its benefits. If he mounted an expedition, he'd conquer one of his own fears—Everest. Not that he was afraid of the climb, because Mal was certain he could make a good attempt at the summit. But he'd never been able to face the emotional toll of that trip. The mountain had killed his father. How could he ever put that aside and focus just on the climb?

And then there was the publicity that the story would bring. Hundreds of thousands of readers subscribed to the magazine, and the Quinn name would be all over the cover and the interior. He'd heard other guides talk about the value of that kind of exposure. It would mean a huge and almost immediate increase in bookings.

The third benefit had nothing at all to do with business. If Amy wrote the article she'd come for, they'd have more time together. Maybe she would still leave the day after tomorrow, but she'd be back. They'd speak on the phone and he might visit New York to work on plans for the Everest expedition.

He couldn't promise her forever. He still wasn't convinced that he led the kind of life that allowed for a wife and family. But right now, Mal needed to be reassured that this all wouldn't just end when she left.

He leaned forward and set the laptop on the other rocker, then struggled to get to his feet, tucking the crutches under his arms. Duff followed him into the house and he headed to the kitchen. He found Amy staring into the bottom of a steaming pot, the scent of onions and garlic and frying sausage permeating he air.

He wrapped his arm around her waist and kissed her cheek.

"What did you think?"

"It was amazing," he said. "It was so...personal. I guess I didn't expect you to reveal yourself that way."

"I didn't, either," Amy said. "But writing it was cathartic. I've been dealing with my inadequacy issues for a long time and now I feel like I've finally conquered them."

"What does that mean?" Mal asked. Was she thinking about leaving her job? Walking away from her last attempt to please her father?

"I'm not sure. I guess I haven't figured it all out right now."

"I'm not sure the story is right for *High Adventure*," Mal said.

Amy nodded. "I know. I realized that when I was writing it. But it might sell somewhere else. I believe it's an important story, about facing your fears and overcoming insecurities."

Her attitude confused him. Had she given up on her dream to write for her father's magazine? It was one thing to come to grips with her personal demons, but abandoning her professional goals was something Mal didn't expect. How else could he get her to stay?

"I've been thinking. Maybe we could talk a bit more about the other story."

She stiffened slightly, then turned to face him, a wooden spoon still clutched in her had. "The story about your father?"

"Yeah. I mean, there's no harm in discussing it a little further, is there?"

Amy shook her head. "No. Not at all." She paused. "I did come up with another angle. It might be interesting to write about your father's death but then talk about how the tragedy has affected everyone twenty years later. His family, his friends, the climbing community. He's still such a legend and it would be like having a memorial service for him. And we could get opinions on whether there should be an expedition to Everest. You know, Innis would probably back off if everyone was against it. Or if they believed that you and your brothers should be the ones to decide."

"I talked to my mum at the hospital," Mal said. "About the expedition. About the three of us climbing Everest and holding a memorial service for my dad up there. About retrieving his last journal."

"What did she say?"

"She said it was up to us," Mal replied. "She didn't exactly give us her blessing, but she said she wouldn't try to stop us anymore."

"Does that mean you're going to do it?"

Mal sighed. "It's so much more complicated than a yes or no answer, Amy. I have to talk to my brothers, I have to figure out what it might mean to the business. And I'm not sure I *want* to do it. So I don't have any answers for you right now. But I do know that I'm going to stop Roger Innis from getting his hands on that journal."

"How are you going to do that?"

"I'm not sure, but between me and Rogan and Ryan, I'm sure we'll come up with a way."

"I'll get something in *High Adventure,*" Amy said. "I have no idea what it will be, but I'm going to write something about you that they'll buy."

"But they would bite for sure if you did a story about an expedition?"

"Yes, of course."

"More people would read that story," he said.

"It would probably be picked up by major news organizations. You might be invited to appear on some talk shows. It's human interest at its best."

Mal pulled her close, resting his chin on top of her head. "Yeah, that's what I figured. I trust you to do it right."

"But you have to give me the exclusive. I read my email this morning—my editor put another writer on the story. He's a hack and he'll turn it into a sensationalistic piece of crap."

"Dana said there's been another guy from *High Adventure* calling the office. I wondered what that was about."

She leaned back and looked up into his eyes. "What do you want to do?"

"I'm going to have to think about it."

"Is the second idea, the memorial article, something you'd consider? Because, if it is, I could interview your mother and sister before I leave."

"I suppose we could go talk to Mum tomorrow. If she agrees, Dana will go along with it. And so will Rogan and Ryan."

"All right," Amy said. "Tomorrow, then." She returned to her dinner preparations, then glanced over her shoulder. "I bought a bottle of wine. Why don't you open it and pour a couple of glasses, then sit down in the living room. I'll be done with this in a few minutes."

Mal searched through the drawer for the corkscrew and when he found it, he opened the bottle. But carrying the wine and the glasses into the other room was impossible with crutches. So he leaned the crutches against the refrigerator and hopped to the couch.

He poured himself a glass, then one for Amy, before taking a long sip of the Australian Pinot. This was lovely, spending the afternoon with Amy, watching her make dinner for the two of them, enjoying a glass of wine. This was what life could be like.

He had the means to make her stay. Now he just needed to convince himself that it was the right thing to do. Did he love her? Could he offer her the kind of life she wanted? Or was he being selfish, interested only in his own happiness even it meant she got hurt in the end?

AMY SLOWLY STIRRED the pot of spaghetti sauce, her mind mulling over the possibility of writing a different kind of story. Did Mal really want to open up his life to the media? Or was he doing this for her? Why?

It was clear that he felt a deep affection for her, as she did for him. And he was right that the story she'd written would never make it into *High Adventure*. But for the other story, he'd have to be the one to convince his family to participate; it would have to be about the whole family, not just him. And he'd said he trusted her to do the article right.

She smiled to herself. They'd grown so close in such a short time. Even if the other story didn't happen, she'd done what she'd come here to do. She'd dealt with the emotional issues of her childhood and had managed to leave them behind. Both her heart and her soul were finally healthy.

She set the cover on the pot, then grabbed the toasted bread from the oven, arranging it on a plate. Amy covered each slice with a chopped tomato mixture, then reached into her pocket and slid the small plastic package beneath one of the slices.

A smile touched her lips. They only had a few days left together. She intended to make the most of them. And that included serving herself up, along with the appetizer course.

She opened the buttons on her blouse until the maximum amount of cleavage was exposed. Then she pulled the elastic band from her haphazard ponytail, shaking out her shoulder-length hair. Though she smelled like fried meat, she knew that the scent was one of Mal's favorites. Who needed perfume to lure a lover when you had hamburger?

Amy grabbed the plate and walked into the living room. Mal was engrossed in a video game and barely looked up at first. But then his gaze followed her as she walked around the coffee table and sat down next to him.

She held out the plate as his video character exploded on the screen. The game stopped and his eyes drifted down to her breasts.

"What is this?" he murmured.

"Bruschetta. It's bread toasted with olive oil and rubbed with garlic. And fresh tomatoes with basil and oil and balsamic vinegar."

"I had balsamic vinegar in the kitchen?"

She shook her head. "No, I bought a bottle at the store."

"Hmm," he said, picking up a piece of bread. "Good on ya." Mal took a bite of the bread and groaned softly. "Oh, my God, this is really good. You are such a fabulous cook." He took another bite, licking his lips as he chewed. "I could eat this all night long."

Mal grabbed another, then froze when he saw the condom package underneath it. He reached out and picked it up. "What's this?"

"Dessert?" Amy said.

He nodded, his sly smile growing wider as he swallowed. "What if I like to eat my dessert before my meal?"

"Only very bad boys do that," Amy said.

Mal set the plate down, but held on to the condom. "I'm a very bad boy. Very, very bad. Are you going to feed me my dessert?"

Amy slowly stood, then straddled his legs, pinning him to the sofa. He had trouble maneuvering with the heavy cast on his leg, but they'd already learned that sex worked much better with her on top.

His gaze fixed on a spot between her breasts. "You're not wearing a bra," he said.

"I haven't had one on all day." She pulled her skirt up around her thighs. "I don't have any panties on, either."

His eyebrows shot up. "How did that get by me? I'm a pathetic excuse for a man."

"I have a way you can redeem yourself," she said, rising up on her knees. She reached down and unzipped his jeans, then grabbed the waistband and tugged. Mal lifted his hips and she managed to pull them down until his shaft was exposed.

He was already getting hard, and Amy reached between them and began to stroke him gently. Mal closed his eyes and tipped his head back. "Brilliant idea," he murmured. "Dinner and exercise all in one shot."

When he was completely hard, Amy opened the condom and smoothed it over his shaft. Then, sliding forward, she positioned herself above him, the tip of his erection teasing at her damp entrance.

Slowly, she lowered herself on top of him, taking him in, inch by inch, until he was buried deeply in her warmth. He clutched at her hips and held her still for a long time, as if he needed to fight for control.

Amy wasn't sure how it was possible, but every time they made love, it felt better than the last. She couldn't understand how anyone could grow bored with sex when there were so many different options. But then, she'd always been rather indifferent about the act, too, until she'd met Mal. He seemed to have an unusual enthusiasm for the sport that was highly contagious.

Maybe it was also the way he made her feel, as if she was the only woman in the world who could satisfy him completely. She barely even thought about the other women he'd had. They didn't matter. What was important was how they were together, this incredibly intense connection that they shared.

Mal loosened his grip on her hips and she took the cue and began to move. His fingers found the buttons of her blouse and he undid them, one by one, until he could caress her breasts. When he tugged the garment down, she slipped out of the sleeves and tossed it aside.

He teased at her nipple with his tongue, then drew it into his mouth, sucking gently until the tip was swollen and hard. Amy watched him through half-closed eyes, enjoying the riot of sensation that pulsed through her body.

She'd learned to surrender to those feelings, channeling them into her need. Closing her eyes, she focused on the feel of him moving inside of her, of his shaft creating a delicious friction that sent her closer and closer to her release.

And when she shifted above him, the torment became even more exquisite, her body beginning to tingle in anticipation. She smoothed her hands over the scruff on his cheeks, then attacked his mouth in a desperate kiss.

He sensed that she was close and when he slowed his pace, she knew he wanted to delay the inevitable. But it was too late for her. She could already feel the wonderful build inside of her, the certainty that pleasure was just a heartbeat away.

Amy pulled his hands from her hips and pinned them on either side of his head, leaning forward until his shaft rubbed against her in just the right way. He surrendered control to her, unable to stop her from finding what she sought.

Her orgasm overwhelmed her, like a rogue wave crashing against her and pulling her under. Shudders coursed through her body, stealing her breath and making her heart pound. It was a long and exhilarating fall, and when she finally touched down, Amy collapsed against him, her lips pressed to the curve of his neck.

He held her, smoothing his hands over her back. And then he drove into her once more and surrendered to his own release. Amy smiled to herself. The man could control himself when he set his mind to it. He always put her pleasure first.

"I do believe you are the best lover I've ever had," she said with a deep sigh.

"How many have you had?"

"Not many." She sat up. "What about you?"

"I don't remember. They all faded into the past the moment I saw you."

A laugh burst from her throat. "Oh, good answer. And a very deft deflection of my question."

"A lot fewer than you'd think," he said. "Since I don't mess around on the job, and I spend most of my time on the job, it doesn't leave much room for women."

"All right, I'll accept that answer."

"They were nothing compared to you. Just sex. No... connection."

Amy tucked his hair behind his ear, wondering what he meant by *connection*. Was he referring to the physical or the emotional bond between them? They seemed to be equally powerful. But she'd been aware from the start that Mal Quinn kept his emotions out of the equation. Had that changed?

This was the problem with charming men, Amy mused. It was impossible to tell what they were really thinking. They used their charm to create a false sense of affection, making a woman believe that there was a deep emotion—love—behind the desire.

But Amy knew better than to assign emotions to a man as smooth and experienced with women as Mal. Until he actually admitted he was madly in love, she'd keep her own declarations in check. Though she was sure he felt something for her, would he confess those feelings before she left? Or would she always wonder if she'd walked away too soon?

"You know, a bloke could starve to death with you around to distract him."

"Are you hungry?"

"Not for food. All my appetites have been completely satisfied."

"I'm good at that," Amy said with a grin.

"You're probably good at everything you do."

It was nice to hear that there was one person in the world who appreciated her for the person she was. Mal Quinn was a man she could easily love. But until he accepted that he could love her, too, falling for him would only lead to heartache.

THEY LEFT EARLY the next morning at the break of dawn.

Mal had decided that they ought to make the best of their last full day and night together before he delivered her to the airport. They'd already returned her rental.

He still hadn't decided whether he'd ask her to stay, but as their time dwindled down, Mal knew he needed to make a decision or risk losing her forever. But maybe a clean break now was for the best. She understood well what a life with him would entail. Her father had been absent from her life. And with him, she'd have a husband who spent ten months of the year away from home.

On the other hand, he probably could afford to make a few concessions in his professional life. His two brothers were still unattached, so they might be able to pick up a bit of the slack. And the company had begun to accumulate some good guides who were more than capable of leading expeditions. Maybe if he was home more he could focus on marketing and sales, increasing their client base and making the business more profitable.

Mal had always wondered if he was spreading himself too thin, trying to juggle too many balls at once.

Maybe this accident had happened for a reason, so he had the time to figure out what he needed to do. Maybe it was fate taking a hand in his life.

He glanced over at Amy, the wind whipping at her pale hair. She'd had to drive. He couldn't sit behind the wheel for more than a half hour without his leg cramping from the angle of the cast.

"Aren't you going to ask where we're going?" he called.

She shrugged, her eyes fixed on the road ahead. "I figured it was supposed to be a surprise. And I enjoy your surprises."

They stopped at a roadside café on the way into Auckland and Amy devoured a huge breakfast. Though Mal warned her that she may want to eat light, she couldn't resist the hotcakes, loaded with strawberries and whipped cream.

An hour later, they cruised into Auckland on the motorway. The moment she saw the first sign, she smiled. "Are we going to visit your mother?"

"Yes," Mal said. "She's agreed to talk with you before you leave. But there's something else that we have to do first."

Mal gave her directions as they drove toward the harbor, then pointed her to an exit. They found the car park and when she pulled the car to a stop, her eyes came to rest on a nearby sign.

"Bungee," she said. "I know this place. The magazine did a feature on it a few years ago."

"Yeah?" Mal said. "This is your big test. I know that you don't like heights, but you've already conquered so many of your fears. If you can do this, there's nothing left to prove."

The climb had been a challenge, but he had been there to guide her. She'd have to do this all on her own. He couldn't hold her hand or make her jump.

"Wow, that's a big bridge," she said.

"Yes," Mal countered. "A little history—commercialized bungee jumping originated in New Zealand, right here in Auckland. A. J. Hackett. He was a good friend of my dad's. He owns this jump. You can't make a trip to this country and not try it."

"And I suppose you're going to beg off because of your broken leg."

Mal nodded. "I'm afraid so. But I will walk out there with you."

"What if I don't want to do it?" she asked.

"It's up to you. But I think you'll really enjoy it. And you didn't have too big a breakfast, so you probably won't break the line."

She reached over and punched his shoulder. "If you think you can tease me into jumping, don't bother." Amy drew a deep breath and let it out. "I'll try it."

Mal wasn't sure why this was suddenly so important to him. Maybe if she had a taste of adventure, she'd understand why he couldn't give it up for the white-picket fence. "You have to go for the water touch," he said. "That's the most fun."

"But then I'll get my hair wet."

Mal shook his head. "That's the point. You have to touch the water."

"Sure, I'd love to resemble a drowned rat when I have lunch with your mother."

He leaned over and stole a quick kiss. "You'd be pretty no matter what your hair looked like."

"Oh, and now with the compliments. Are you sure you don't want to use all that charm to get me out of my clothes instead of making me jump off a bridge?"

Mal opened the door. "Come on, let's go."

They walked to the office, Mal on crutches and Amy a few steps behind. Mal held the door as Amy stepped inside. He recognized two of the jump technicians and gave them a wave. They walked over and shook his hand.

"Hey there, Jerry. Sam. How are you?"

"What happened to your leg?" Sam asked.

"I broke it. Stepped wrong on a climb a few days ago. It'll be good in about six weeks, they say." He turned to Amy. "Amy, this is Sam Belling and Jerry Warner. They've worked with me as guides on some of our back-country trips. They're going to be the guys who'll push you off the bridge."

"No, no, no," the pair said in tandem. "We never push. We may cajole, but there's never any pushing."

"Glad to hear it," Amy said. "So what do I have to do to get this done?"

"Come with me," Jerry said. "I'll get you all signed up."

"Here," Mal said, handing him a bank card. "Get a ticket for me, too. I want to watch."

Mal and Sam stayed behind as the pair walked away. "American?" Sam asked.

"Yeah. New York. She works for *High Adventure* magazine."

"No shit? I love that magazine. We were in it last

year. They did a whole profile on New Zealand bungee jumping and A.J. brought in a lot of business from the Yank tourists." He glanced down at Mal's leg. "We usually wouldn't let you out on the catwalk with those crutches, but since you're an old friend of the owner, you're cool. Just don't trip and fall into the water."

"The rock crumbled," he said.

"Yeah, yeah. I'd be tripping and falling all over myself, too, if I had that sweet thing to chase after. Nice bum."

Amy turned back from the counter, her expression uneasy. Jerry handed her a helmet and she held it up and pointed to it, a bemused expression on her face. Then she stepped into her harness and joined the four other customers who were standing in a semicircle, listening to instructions.

When the jumpers had been prepped, they each stepped on a scale to have their weights recorded before they climbed onto the catwalk that would take them out to the center of the bridge.

"Let's go," Sam said. "I don't want to miss all the terror and tears."

"You don't think she'll do it?" Mal asked.

"Oh, she'll do it, all right," Sam replied. "I was talking about you."

They followed the group out onto the catwalk, making their way beneath the bridge until they reached the jump pod. The jumpers waited while the technicians hooked up the bungees and checked all the fittings.

"All right," Jerry said. "Who'll go first?"

"I will," Amy said, raising her hand.

"All right, then," Sam said, winking at Mal. "Step

right up. Do you want to take the dip and get wet or would you like to stay dry?"

"Oh, what the hell," Amy said. "Let's do the whole nine yards."

"And that would be?" Jerry asked.

"Wet."

Mal moved to the rail as Amy was attached to the bungee. "Are you sure about this?" he said to her.

"Positive," she said.

He grinned and gave her the thumbs-up. She gave him one last nervous glance as she stepped onto the platform and looked down at the water. Then she drew a deep breath, closed her eyes, held out her arms and fell forward.

Mal watched as she dropped toward the water, almost as if she was floating down like a feather instead of falling like a stone. She hit the surface and immediately bounced back up, then quickly dropped again. He could hear her screaming and he wondered if they were screams of fear or exhilaration.

To his relief she was laughing when they hauled her into the pod again. The moment she was unhooked from the cable, she ran over to him and threw herself into his arms. "That was so much fun. It was like flying. Do you think they'd let me do it again?"

Mal caught her chin, then kissed her, their arms wrapped around each other. The rest of the world just faded into gray and Mal held on to her as if he never wanted to let her go. And now he wasn't sure he could.

Tonight, he'd ask her to stay, at least until his ankle

healed. After that, he'd go back to the life of an adventurer, and she deserved more than that. But he could offer her a few more months.

9

THE PHONE WOKE Amy from a deep sleep and for a moment, she wasn't sure where she was. She squinted at the light coming through the window and rubbed her eyes, then heard a voice from behind her say, "Are you going to answer that or should I?

She smiled. Mal. They were here in a hotel room, in Auckland. She'd decided to blow the rest of her New Zealand budget on a luxury room in the Skycity Grand in the center of Auckland.

After her jump, they'd had a pleasant lunch with Lydie Quinn. They talked for nearly an hour and Amy had walked away with a solid idea for a story about Max Quinn that Lydie and the family were happy with. She also was more determined than ever to sell the family on a biography. Max had led such a colorful and exciting life. It deserved its own story.

After they left Lydie's condo, Amy and Mal checked into the hotel. They'd tumbled into bed, emerging from the room for a nice dinner and then heading back for another "nap."

"Do you want me to answer it?"

"I didn't leave a wake-up call. And no one knows we're here."

Groaning, Mal rolled over her, his cast scraping along her leg. She winced as he picked up the phone. "Hello."

Amy listened to Mal's end of the conversation, then he handed her the phone. "It's your father," he said.

"Who?"

"Your father. He wants to talk to you."

"No," she said, pushing Mal off her and scrambling out of bed. She grabbed up one of the plush robes that the hotel provided and quickly wrapped it around her. "No, I don't want to talk to him."

Mal shrugged. "I'm sorry, she doesn't want to talk to you." He paused. "No, I'm quite sure I explained that it was you.…Yes. That's entirely up to you.…Who am I? I'm a friend. A very close friend.…All right. Good-bye, then."

Mal hung up the phone and flopped back down into the pillows. "My initial impression of him was correct. He is a horse's arse."

"What did he want?" Amy asked. "And how did he find out I was here?"

"He didn't say. Just that he wanted to talk to you. And I suspect he has a trace on your credit card. You used it to pay for the room, didn't you?"

Amy cursed to herself. It wasn't *her* credit card. It was a card her mother had given her, a card that her father probably paid for. "Yeah. But why would he want to track me down here?"

Mal reached for the phone and pulled it out of the cradle, then held it out to her. "Call him back and ask."

She snatched the phone out of his hand and slammed it down again. "No. I don't want to talk to him. I don't have anything to say to him, no matter what he has to say to me."

For the first time in her life, she didn't care what her father had to say or what he thought of her. As if a great weight had been lifted from her soul, Amy realized that he didn't matter anymore. She didn't need to please him or prove herself to him. She was a strong, compassionate, clever woman and if he couldn't appreciate that, then it was his loss.

But there was one man who did appreciate her. And he was lying in bed next to her. Amy raked her fingers through her hair. She drew a deep breath and then another realization hit her. "Oh, my God, what if something happened to my mom? Did he say it was an emergency?"

"No," Mal said, pushing up on his elbows. "Amy, I'm sure if it was an emergency, he would have said something to me. Besides, wouldn't he have left a message on your cell?"

"You said it yourself. He's an ass. Did he want me to call him back?"

"Yes, he said that he'd be in his office for another two hours."

"Which office? He has about twenty."

"I believe he said his Los Angeles office."

She sat down on the edge of the bed. "I wonder what time it is in New York. I should try my mom. If it's not her, then I'll be able to relax and forget his call."

Mal rubbed his forehead. "It's late afternoon in New York. Probably about four or five p.m. yesterday."

"I'm going to call her," Amy said. She snatched up the phone and handed it to him. "How do I do that?"

Mal rang the switchboard and requested that they dial for Amy, then handed her the phone. She walked over to the sitting area and sat down on the sofa, tucking her feet beneath her. After about thirty seconds, her expression brightened.

"Mama?…Hi! It's Amy.…No, I'm still in New Zealand. I'm leaving later tonight. I just wanted to say that I'll call you when I get home. I've missed you.…Oh, it's been wonderful. I've done so many exciting things.… The story? I'll explain that all to you when I see you. Okay, I have to go. Take care. Love you."

She switched off the phone, then collapsed into the soft cushions of the sofa. "Everything is fine with her," she said. "Okay. I'm good. Why don't we order some breakfast and figure out what we're going to do for the rest of the day?"

"I know exactly what I want to do," he said. "I want to stay here in this bed with you until the very last minute."

Amy crossed the room and crawled back on the bed. "Then we'd better order you a big breakfast so that you have plenty of energy."

He grabbed her arm and yanked her onto the bed with him, rolling her beneath him—and then cursed. Though the cast protected the break, it was still painful when he moved the wrong way.

"Be careful," she said.

He stared down into her eyes. "This from the woman

who has been so careful. The woman who climbed a mountain and walked down on her own to rescue me. The woman who jumped off a bridge."

"I guess things have changed a little bit," she murmured, her gaze falling to his mouth. She bent closer and kissed him, his lips warm against hers.

"Yes, they have. A lot has changed."

"I'm going to miss you," she murmured.

"You don't have to miss me," he said, reaching up. "You could always stay." Mal ran his thumb along her bottom lip. "I'm asking you to stay."

She frowned, his words not registering at first. What was he saying? Did he just want her to stay *longer,* or stay *forever?* His invitation was so vague. Maybe he intended it to be vague. And if it was, maybe he really wasn't completely sure of what he wanted himself.

But how could she be certain of what she wanted if he wasn't certain? Amy's mind spun with all the possible questions and all the myriad answers he might give. "I—I don't know. I suppose we could talk about it."

"There's nothing to talk about," Mal said. "I'm saying I want you to stay. And now you can say one of two things. Either you want to stay or you don't."

"It's not that simple," Amy said.

"Yes, it is," Mal quickly countered. "It's as simple as can be."

"Why do you want me to stay?"

"Because I don't want you to leave," Mal replied.

Amy shook her head. Was he being deliberately obtuse or was this some sort of game he was playing to get her to admit her feelings for him before he admitted them to her? "Let me pose a hypothetical question."

Mal groaned and pulled the pillow over his face. "No, not a hypothetical. I never get these right."

"If we were in a hotel room in New York and you had a ticket to go back home in eight hours and I asked you to stay, what would you say?"

He sighed. "You're right, it's not a simple answer. But I don't want this to end. And if that means you stay, then I'll be the happiest guy in the world. And if you tell me that you have to leave but that we'll see each other again soon, then I'll try to be happy with that. But I don't want you to leave here and never think about us again."

"That's impossible," she said. "Give me some time?"

"Sure," Mal said. "But you only have eight hours, so you don't have that long." He gave her a sweet smile and Amy realized he held her heart. He was the most wonderful man she'd ever met. Why was it so difficult to say yes?

She already knew the answer to that, though. She needed to hear him tell her that he loved her. So that she'd be sure there was something more than just lust behind his offer.

Then that was her decision. If he told her that he loved her before she left, then she'd stay. If not, she'd go. Nothing less would keep her in New Zealand.

A knock sounded at the door and she looked over at Mal. "Are you expecting company?"

"No," he said. "Maybe it's a free breakfast?"

She walked to the door and opened it. A bellman was standing in the hall with an envelope. "Miss Engalls? This arrived just a few moments ago. It's marked urgent."

Amy took the envelope from his hands. "Thank you," she murmured.

She closed the door and walked back to the bed.

"What is it?" Mal asked.

"I'm not sure."

She sat down on the end of the bed and opened the envelope. Scanning the text, her eyes came to rest on the name at the bottom. Richard Engalls. Her eyes drifted up to the top and she read the body of the letter.

When she finished, she took a deep breath. She should have known. Just when she'd finally figured out her life, another complication had popped up.

Her father was offering her a deal. If she got the story on Max Quinn and his sons and managed to arrange an Everest expedition involving the three Quinns, her father would make her an editor at whatever magazine she chose.

Amy wadded up the paper and tossed it across the room, missing the wastebasket by a few feet. "I need to take a shower," she said, standing up. "Would you order breakfast? I'm really hungry."

THE SOUND OF the shower filtered through the bathroom door. Mal sat on the edge of the bed, his eyes fixed on the crumpled paper sitting against the wall. He wanted to go over and pick it up, but he knew it was none of his business.

If she wanted to tell him what it said, then she would. Whatever it was, it hadn't made her happy.

He pushed out of bed and hopped across the room to grab his crutches, then hobbled over to the bathroom door. He tested the knob and found it unlocked. Mal pushed it open and walked inside, then leaned against the edge of the sink.

When she pulled the shower curtain back and saw him, she jumped in shock, pressing her hand to her chest. "You scared me."

"What was in the note?" he said.

She stepped out of the tub and pulled on her dressing gown, then grabbed a fresh towel and brushed by him, her hair still dripping water. "It isn't important."

"It's bothering you, so that makes it important to me," he said, following her.

"Then read it." She bent down and retrieved the paper and tossed it at him. "It's quite an interesting proposal."

Mal sank down on the bed and smoothed the paper out on his lap, then read it slowly. When he was finished, he stared up at her. Tears glittered in her eyes and his heart ached at the pain in her expression. "Like I said," he murmured, "your father is an ass."

She cursed softly. "He could have promoted me because I've done a good job for the magazine for the past five years. Or because I'm an outstanding writer. But he promises to promote me because suddenly I can finally do something for him." She faced the mirror and began to rub the moisture from her hair with the towel, her movements sharp and angry. "That's how it always is with him. It's all about money and never about love. My brother figured that out years ago, it's just taken me a little longer. But I've got it now."

"Isn't it about time you stopped caring, Amy? You can't make him love you the way you deserve to be loved. He's a bad father and nothing you do is going to magically turn him into some ideal daddy."

"I know, I know. I've come to grips with his… inadequacies. And now I've also realized that maybe I've been working at that magazine just hoping that he'd finally recognize my value and promote me. But now that he has, I don't want it."

"Your job?"

"No, his approval. I like my job. I'm good at it. And I would be a great features writer, too. So maybe it's time I took the initiative and asked for a promotion."

"And if they say no?"

"I'll quit," she said. "I climbed a freakin' mountain. I jumped off a bridge. I can certainly find myself a new job."

"But what if you didn't?" Mal suggested. "If becoming an editor is really that important to you, then you should give him the story he wants."

She laughed bitterly. "And how would that work?"

Mal shrugged. "Maybe I can convince my brothers to participate. It's Everest. None of us have ever climbed Everest. We could retrieve the journal and have a memorial. And if your father is going to finance it, why not try?"

"No. He's going to make it all about him. He'll turn it into one big media circus about how magnanimous he is. And you couldn't control it. It would be…unseemly."

"But it would get you what you want," Mal said.

"At what expense? Hurting your mother? Embarrassing your brothers and you? I'm not going to be part of that." She snatched the paper from his hands and wadded it back into a ball. "Forget it."

"He would be better than Roger Innis," Mal said. "We don't have the money to stop Innis. He'll tramp up that mountain and get exactly what he wants and he'll make himself look like the hero. And no one will question his motives. At least your father is honest about what he wants. He's got no ulterior motives beyond good press for himself."

"No," she said. "I'm not going to do this for him. I don't want the story. You don't need the story." She tossed the towel aside, then sat next to him. She took his hand in hers and laced her fingers through his. "I don't want to spend the rest of the day arguing about this. I want to remember all the fun we had. And I want to have a little more fun. And then I'm going to cry a little bit and say goodbye."

That was it, Mal thought to himself. She had no intention of staying. She had no reason to stay. She didn't want to do the story anymore. He drew in a long, slow breath. So it was what he'd always believed it to be—a short but very sweet affair. One with a beginning and an end. Isn't that what he wanted?

"All right," Mal said. "What do you want to do?"

"You're the adventure guide, Mr. Quinn. I'll leave that up to you. We have to check out by eleven."

"Well, because of this bloody cast I have to drag around, we might just want to have a relaxing day. Perhaps a lot of sitting? And eating? Breakfast at a nice café, good coffee and a chance to talk about everything we haven't talked about yet. And then lunch, a bottle of wine and more talk. And dinner? Maybe a place down near the water."

She nodded. "We're going to eat our way through the day? That sounds like a wonderful idea."

Mal agreed. It was better than spending the day in bed and knowing it might be last time they ever touched each other again. "When does your plane leave?"

"Nine-thirty. But I need to be there by seven."

"Then we have ten hours. I'm going to take a quick shower and shave and you're going to get dressed and then we'll go. And we can leave your bags here. I'm going to stay another night and drive home tomorrow. I think I might want to have a few drinks after you leave."

She crawled onto his lap and wrapped her arms around his neck. "Or maybe we should just order room service and stay in the room until I have to go."

"That's an interesting option, too," he said, pulling her down onto the bed.

"So do we start with breakfast or your shower?"

"Are you going to join me in the shower?"

"I'm clean," she said.

"But I have a broken leg and I need someone to wash my back and my chest and my hair. When I was in the hospital, I had a very naughty nurse. She knew exactly what to do to make me feel better."

"Oh, you are really using this injury for all you can get, aren't you?"

He slipped his fingers down the neck of her dressing down, gently pulling it apart until he could see the soft flesh of her breasts. Mal leaned in and pressed a kiss on her cleavage. "I just like the way you take care of me," he said.

"Maybe you should take care of me now," Amy said. She stood up and leaned over him, resting her arms on his shoulders. "We could play naughty bellman. Why don't you go out into the hall and knock on the door and we'll see what develops."

"Naughty bellboy in a dressing gown with crutches?"

"I have a very good imagination."

Mal stood up, glad that he'd managed to coax her out of her dark mood. Screw Richard Engalls. And screw any other father who couldn't be bothered to love his daughter. Amy deserved so much more from the men in her life. And if he was lucky enough to become one of them, then he would show her how much she was worth every single day for the rest of her life. But he wouldn't be there every day of her life, would he? He'd be on some glacier or mountain with total strangers.

AMY CURLED UP into Mal's naked body, her fingers slowly drifting up and down his broad chest. She drew in a deep breath, taking in his scent and committing it to memory. How would she ever live without this? In less than two weeks, she'd become a wanton sex goddess and Malcolm Quinn had been her teacher.

Would she ever be able to find another man who could satisfy her in bed the way he could? And it wasn't just about the sex, she thought, although the sex was a big part of it. It was the way they just seemed to fit.

If anyone had told her she'd have a passionate affair with Mal on this trip, she would have laughed them out of the room. What could a man like Mal ever find interesting in a woman like her? But he'd shown her that it wasn't about exotic looks or a hot body. Sexual attraction was about chemistry. Two stable elements that when combined became volatile. Explosive.

"I can hear you thinking," he said.

"What time is it?"

"We have to leave in an hour."

She sat up and brushed the hair out of her eyes. "Maybe I should just take a cab. Then I can say good-bye to you here and there won't be any public crying or emotional breakdowns in the drop-off zone."

She prayed that he'd agree. Leaving was going to be almost impossible already. Why make it more difficult?

"All right," he murmured. "If that's what you want, then that's what we'll do."

"Thank you," she said.

"You're welcome." He pulled her back down next to him, wrapping his arm around her shoulder and playing with a strand of her hair. "So what don't I know about you that I should? I think we need to fill this last hour with details. Tell me about your first kiss."

"Oh, dear. Are these questions designed to show you what an absolute failure I was in high school?"

"Answer it," he urged.

"It was senior prom. Gordy Ross. Tall, skinny, a moustache that looked like a caterpillar stuck to his upper lip. He kissed me, but it tickled and I laughed. He got mad and took me home early."

"Ouch."

"Now you. How did you lose your virginity?"

"I was sixteen, she was eighteen. I was convinced I knew everything there was to know about sex and that I could show her a good time. Turns out, she knew a lot more than me and I walked away with a great appreciation for what a girl could do with her tongue."

"Ah," Amy said. "Maybe you could give me her

name and I'll write her a thank-you note for turning you into such a devoted student of seduction." She snuggled closer, resting her head on his chest. "We don't really know each other very well, do we?"

"No, I suppose we don't."

"I guess it's for the best that it's ending now. We'll never get bored with each other this way."

"I suppose we won't."

A long silence grew between them and she listened to his heart beating, sure and strong. If only that heart could speak. What was he feeling? Did he have anything beyond simple affection for her?

She had the courage to ask him, to put the question out there on the table. But she couldn't handle the rejection if it came. They'd had a wonderful time together—two weeks that she'd remember for the rest of her life. Mal Quinn would be the example that every subsequent man in her life would be measured against.

The last thing she wanted was those memories tainted with hurt and humiliation. Amy would rather walk away than risk that. Hell, she'd had enough of that from her father. She'd never been able to make him love her, and the same could be said for Mal. If he really wanted her, he'd tell her.

Or maybe she should take one more risk. She groaned inwardly. This was where true courage came into play. And Amy wasn't sure that she possessed a lot of that. Though it was easy to put on a brave face for Mal, there was still a tiny part of her that was that rejected little girl. Would that ever go away?

"I should probably pack," she said. "I've got to find my ticket and passport." Amy untangled her limbs from his and crawled out of bed, slipping into the robe before gathering her things from around the room.

Most of her clothes were packed in her larger suitcase, so she opened her overnight bag and began to re-arrange the contents.

"What airline are you flying?" Mal asked.

"Air New Zealand to L.A., and then I think it's United to Newark."

"Where is Newark?"

"New Jersey," she said. "It was the cheapest flight I could get. I figured if I didn't get the story at least it wouldn't have spent a lot for the failure."

"I told you, we could try to do the story."

"No. It's not important now. And to be honest, since I've met your mother, I really wouldn't want to put her through it. It was a bad idea from the beginning."

"What are you going to do when you get home?" he asked.

"I'm going to find someone to buy my story. The one about our climb. I'm sure I can find a magazine that would be interested. Maybe even an airline magazine. They pay pretty well."

"If it gets published, I want you to send me a copy."

Amy nodded. "I will."

She shrugged out of the robe and pulled on the pink underwear she'd worn that night in the hospital. Then she tugged a comfortable cotton knit dress over her head and let it drop down over her body.

"That's pretty," Mal said. "I've never seen you wear that."

"It's my traveling dress. It's stretchy and comfy and the skirt is long enough to keep my legs warm."

"I should have given you the fleece you wore on our climb. That's what I usually wear on planes."

Amy sat down next to him and smoothed her hand over his brow. "Are you going to be able to get back home on your own with your leg?"

Mal nodded. "I can drive. I'll just have to stop every now and then to stretch it out."

"All right."

"I'm going to walk down to the cab with you," he said. "It just doesn't seem right that I don't see you safely into the car. I got you up a mountain, I'll get you into a cab."

"You don't have to do that," she said.

"But I want to." He got out of bed then, hopping on one foot, and found his clothes. She took one last chance to admire his naked body, finding all the little spots that she'd explored and wondering who might explore them next.

Mal would never lack for female companionship. He'd come into the pub the day they'd met looking to get laid. And he'd done exactly that. Someday, in the not-too-distant future, he'd walk into that pub again and there would be another woman, and he'd charm her and take her home to his bed. And maybe they would live happily ever after.

"Before we leave, I have something for you," he said.

"What is it?"

Mal grabbed his duffel and withdrew a flat package, then handed it to her. "It's nothing important."

With trembling fingers, Amy opened it, tearing away the paper and lifting the lid off the box. Inside was a picture frame with the photo of the two of them on the summit of Mount French, their arms raised. It was a selfie, but with Mal's long arms, he'd been able to get a good deal of the background in—the blue sky and the peaks behind them.

Amy drew a ragged breath as she stared at the photo. To any stranger, they seemed like the happiest couple in the world. Maybe even a couple who were in love. But to her, it was simply a memory of a perfect day spent with a wonderful man. A lover and a friend.

"It's beautiful," she said, running her fingers over the glass. She brought it to her chest and smiled. "I'll treasure it always."

He frowned. "It's just a photo."

"I know," Amy said.

She gave him only a quick kiss, aware that if she lingered over his mouth, she might start to weep big, wet tears. It would be an ugly cry and Amy didn't want him to remember her like that, all red and puffy, her eyes watery and her nose running. She wanted him to remember the woman who drove him crazy in bed, the one who played Naughty Nurse and who seduced him on his living room sofa. The one he couldn't seem to get enough of.

It was time to leave. The longer she waited, the more difficult it would be. Amy forced a smile, then nodded. "We'd better go. I don't want to be late."

10

"I GUESS THIS is it."

They stood outside the hotel, Mal leaning on his crutches as the cab driver loaded Amy's bags into the boot of the taxi. "Yep," Mal said. "It's been fun."

"It has."

She tried to smile, but Mal could see she was having trouble maintaining a bright expression. "Promise you'll give me a ring when you get home safely?"

"I will," she said. "I have your number."

"Perfect. Do you have your ticket? And your passport?"

"Yes. I'm going to kiss you one more time and then I'm going to get in the cab and leave."

"All right," Mal said. He slipped his arm around her waist and pulled her against him. Their lips met, and as it had always been between them, the kiss was perfect, soft and sweet and filled with unexpressed longing.

Mal fought the urge to drag her back upstairs and convince her to stay. But there were too many things standing between them. He couldn't offer her the kind of relationship she deserved. Amy should have a man who was there for her every day, making her smile and laugh, supporting her in everything she did.

A relationship with him would always be about goodbyes, about worrying and waiting for a phone call, having nightmares about disasters and waking up alone night after night. He cared enough about Amy to want more for her.

So this decision was noble; he could convince himself that they would never really have worked out anyway, that he was doing her a favor.

But though all of that might provide some kind of rationalization, it wasn't going to make the pain or the loneliness go away. Every night he'd wish she was beside him in bed, and he'd ache for the touch of her fingers or the taste of her lips. Instead, he'd have to be satisfied with the memories and hope she was happy with another man.

When she finally drew away, he pressed his forehead against hers. "I have to go," she murmured.

"I know. Have a safe trip."

She turned and slipped inside the cab, then closed the door. He stared at her through the tinted glass and gave her a little wave. And then, before he could do anything about it, the cab roared off.

Mal stared at the car as it pulled into traffic and then disappeared. He waited for the ache to set in, for the realization to hit him that he'd let the only woman he'd ever wanted to love get away.

"Never fun saying goodbye, eh?"

The doorman stood beside him, his gloved hands clasped behind his back.

"Never," Mal said.

"That your wife?"

"No," Mal said.

"Fiancée?"

"No."

"Girlfriend, then."

"We're just…just…friends," he finally said.

"Really? I would have bet there was something more than friendship going on there. You didn't have the look of friends."

"All right, *close* friends," Mal conceded. But they'd never been that, had they? He loved her. *He loved her.* "Oh, shit." He glanced down the drive and waved. "I need a cab."

The doorman stepped to the curb and blew his whistle and a cab sped up from the line. He helped Mal get into the car, then slid his crutches in after him. "Good luck." He patted the top of the cab and the driver took off.

"Where to?" the cabbie asked.

"The airport," he said. "There's another cab that left about two minutes ago. If you could catch up to it, that would be great."

"I'll give it a try," the driver said. "Do you know what route they took?"

"No," Mal said.

They wove in and out of the late-evening traffic, taking the motorway out of downtown. But there were a hundred different ways to get to the airport, and Mal didn't hold out much hope that two different cab drivers would take the same route.

But he remembered the airline and that it was an international flight. He'd flown out of Auckland so many times that he knew the airport by heart. If he could catch her before she went through security, then he'd have a chance to tell her what he should have said earlier.

Mal just hadn't realized what it would feel like to lose her. Like his heart had just been ripped out of his chest while it was still beating. Like his lungs had refused to draw air and his brain couldn't put together a logical thought. It was a physical reaction, and one he didn't ever want to experience again.

The trip to the airport was tortuously long. They didn't catch up to Amy's cab, so he had the driver drop him at the Air New Zealand sign in front of the international terminal. He reached for his wallet in his back pocket, then realized he'd left it in the room.

Mal shook his head. If he hadn't been on crutches, he'd make a dash for it. But as it was, there was no way he was going to nick off without getting caught. He leaned in the window and smiled apologetically. "Listen, I don't have any money. I left my wallet back at the hotel, but I swear, I'll pay you just as soon as I take care of some business. If you just wait here for me, we'll ride back to the hotel together and I'll pay you double the regular fare."

The cab driver considered the offer. "You look like a trustworthy bloke."

Mal sighed. "I am. Very trustworthy."

"All right. You'd better hurry if you want to catch her."

Mal managed to get through the sliding doors, but maneuvering through the terminal was going to be slow going on crutches. He noticed a porter standing near a row of luggage trolleys and he approached him.

"I need a wheelchair," he said. "I'm late for my flight."

"Yes, sir. Have you checked in?"

"Yes," Mal said.

"Can you show me your boarding pass?"

"No," he said.

"No? I have to see your boarding pass to—"

"I don't have one," Mal said. "I'm trying to catch up to my girlfriend. She's getting on a flight for the States and I need to tell her that I love her."

"I can get you as far as security, but after that, you'll need a ticket."

"All right," Mal said. "Let's give it a try."

"Wait here." The porter disappeared for a moment, then came driving up in a small cart. "What flight?"

"Air New Zealand to Los Angeles. It leaves at nine-thirty."

"Flight 280," he said. "It's scheduled to leave from Gate 18B. That's on the east concourse." He hit the accelerator and they took off, weaving through the crowds. Whenever they slowed, the porter tooted his horn and the people would part.

Mal searched the crowd for Amy's face, but he didn't see her at all. She couldn't be at the gate yet. Maybe she was still at the baggage check-in.

When they reached security, the porter turned the cart around and they headed back, driving slower so he could carefully examine each person that passed. "I suppose we could ask if she's checked in yet," he said.

"And we could have them call the gate and tell her to come back if she's already gone through security."

"Good idea…"

"Marcus. My name is Marcus."

"I'm Malcolm," he said, holding out his hand.

The porter shook it, then began to steer the cart toward the check-in area, while Mal described in great detail Amy's hair and clothing, the way she walked, the color of her eyes.

It was crowded and the lines of people and baggage made it difficult to navigate. Mal continued his search, but it was as if she'd just disappeared into thin air.

"I'll go from here," he said. "Thank you. I wish I could tip you but—"

"No worries," Marcus said. "Catch me next time." He gave Mal a wave and headed off, his cart horn beeping to part the crowds.

Mal made his way to the front of the line at the Air New Zealand counter and no one seemed to mind. There was a benefit to being on crutches. "Excuse me," he said to the pretty girl attaching tags to luggage. "I need to check on a passenger. Her name is Amy Engalls. She's on the nine-thirty flight to Los Angeles?"

"I'm sorry, sir, I can't give out that information."

"It's an emergency. I have to talk to her before she leaves. I have to— I have to tell her that I love her."

The agent's stern expression softened and the female passenger at the counter sighed. "Oh, that's lovely," the elderly woman said. "Help him, dear, he can't do this on his own. He has a broken leg."

"I don't know what information I can give you," she said. "But I'll try. What's the name?"

"Engalls." Mal spelled it out, then gave the agent the first name. He waited as she typed in a few things, then nodded. "Yes, here she is. She was actually offered an earlier flight because we were overbooked on her flight. I'm afraid she'd already boarded."

"But she just got here."

"Yes, but she was able to go through security quite quickly. I'm afraid she's on her way to…Honolulu."

Mal had never felt so defeated in his life. Not even after a failed summit bid did he experience such utter emotional exhaustion. "Thanks," he murmured.

"Sorry," the agent said.

"No problem." He slowly made his way back to the front doors of the terminal. But a voice stopped him before he could reach the door.

"Mal?"

He slowly turned to find his brother Rogan staring at him. "Hey. You're home."

"Are you here to pick me up? Didn't Dana tell you I'd be staying in town for a few days with Elodie?"

Elodie was one of Rogan's many lady friends, women he slept with on a regular basis but didn't date. She was a flight attendant for Air New Zealand. Wait—

"Do you think Elodie could stop a flight from taking off?"

"Only if she's on board."

So it really was over. "Can I have your wallet? I need some cash."

His brother pulled his wallet out of his back pocket and handed it to Mal. "We have to go find Marcus. I owe him a tip. And my cabbie is waiting outside."

Rogan stared at him as if he'd gone stark raving mad,

but Mal could only feel numb. He'd screwed up and now there was no way to fix it. Somehow he sensed that he'd just made the biggest mistake of his life.

AMY STOOD IN the center of the waiting area, her overnight bag at her feet.

"Ma'am, you have to board now. We can't wait any longer."

She stared mutely at the agent. This was it. Turnaround time. If she didn't make a decision now, her whole life could change. She'd reached the point of no return and the moment she stepped onto the plane, she'd have nothing left but her regrets.

"Are you coming? Ma'am, we can't hold the door any longer."

"No," Amy said in a firm voice. "I'm not going. I can't. I'm sorry."

"You do realize your baggage will be on its way to New York?"

"Yes," Amy said. "That's all right. I'll call my mother and have her pick it up. I'm sorry to keep you waiting."

She spun away from the boarding area and walked toward the concourse. Now that she'd made her decision, she wasn't quite sure what to do. She could take a cab back to the hotel and confront Mal right away. Or she could hang out in the airport, consider her options and then see him in the morning. Or she could sit down right here and have a good cry, then turn around and get on the next flight home before he had a chance to reject her.

No, Amy said to herself. She'd decided to tell him exactly how she felt and she'd deal with his response when she saw it. If he rejected her, she'd be crushed. And if he professed his undying love, she'd be elated.

Quickening her pace, she headed to the exit. She'd return to the hotel and tell him right away. And if he didn't share her feelings, then she would come back to the airport and get on the first available flight home.

"Smart, Amy," she muttered. "You could have just said this all to him earlier and saved yourself all the stress and expense."

Why hadn't she been able to confess her feelings to him? Had it taken walking away from Mal to realize that she might not get a second chance?

When she reached the curb, she dug through her bag for her wallet. She didn't have much cash left. Just enough for the cab fare and a tip, as long as the cabbie took the same route as the driver did coming to the airport.

When a taxi pulled up, she leaned down to speak to the driver. "I have fifty dollars. Is that enough to get me to the Skycity Grand?"

"Should be fine," the driver said.

Amy loaded her carry-on bag into the trunk, then got in the backseat. She collapsed into the soft leather and closed her eyes as the taxi pulled away from the airport.

What would she say to Mal when she finally saw him? Would she just blurt out her feelings, or should she try to compose her words into pretty, romantic phrases?

Maybe she ought to just throw herself into his arms and kiss him. That was always a good start. Once he realized what he'd be missing, then she could make her case.

It was a huge step, starting a new life in New Zealand. She had no friends or family here. She was a half world away from her mother. And she also wouldn't have a job. But Amy felt ready to start anew, to throw herself into a completely different life.

By the time she pulled up at the hotel, it was nearly nine o'clock. She paid the cabbie, unloaded her bag and dragged it to the elevator. When the doors opened, she got inside and went up to the sixth floor.

Their room, 612, was at the end of the hall. When Amy got to the door, she smoothed her hair and pasted a smile on her face. She'd decided to start with a kiss and go from there. But she'd better make it a good one.

Raising her hand, she rapped on the door. When there was no sound from inside, she knocked again. After waiting two or three minutes, she was forced to acknowledge that he wasn't in. He'd probably gone to get some dinner. Maybe he was in the restaurant or the bar.

Amy dragged her suitcase back down to the lobby and stood at the reception desk. After a short wait, a clerk appeared. "How can I help you?"

"I went up to room 612 and Malcolm Quinn wasn't in. I was staying in the room with him last night and he said he was staying there tonight. I expect he might be out for dinner. Can I get a key?"

The clerk tapped on her keyboard, then frowned. "I'm afraid Mr. Quinn has checked out. About fifteen minutes ago. You just missed him."

Amy groaned, her eyes filling with tears. "But he paid for the room?"

"Yes. But he's not staying with us anymore."

"Where did he go?"

"I expect he went home?"

She'd spent the last of her cash on the cab. And she wasn't about to put anything else on her credit card, now that she knew her father was paying for it. She also needed to rent a car and drive to Raglan first thing tomorrow morning.

Amy smoothed her hands over the cool granite countertop. "Is it possible for me to take the room? I—I missed my flight and I came back to spend the night with him and now he's gone. The room *is* already paid for."

The clerk glanced to either side of her, then tapped something else into her computer. "I'll just get you a key card," she whispered.

Amy drew a ragged breath, smiling through her tears. "Thank you."

The clerk slid the card across the granite counter. Amy snatched it up and headed for the elevator. She'd get a decent night's sleep and deal with all of this in the morning.

When she got to the room and opened the door, a flood of memories rushed over her. The bed was still mussed from their afternoon of lovemaking and she could still smell the scent of his shampoo. She set her bag aside and stripped off all her clothes, then crawled between the cool sheets.

With a soft sigh, Amy pulled his pillow over her face and tried to imagine that he was here lying beside her. But his half of the bed was cold and empty.

"I love you," she said, practicing the words out loud. "Malcolm Quinn, I love you. I love you." Amy groaned and covered her face. "I love, love, love you."

How many different ways were there to say those three little words? She'd always expected that when she said them to a man they'd just come naturally and that they'd be quickly reciprocated. But now she had nothing but doubts and there was a good chance that it wouldn't turn out the way she wanted.

Amy closed her eyes and let her mind drift back to all the wonderful times they'd had together, the laughter, the teasing, the passion and the way they couldn't keep their hands off each other. The feelings had been so intense, the connection so perfect. How could he not believe that was love?

She'd know soon enough. Amy rolled over on her stomach and picked up the phone. She dialed the number for the hotel operator.

"I'd like to place a call to the United States." She gave the operator the number, then waited for the phone to ring on the other end. She had no idea what time it was in New York, and it didn't really matter. Right now she needed to talk to her mother.

"Hello?"

"Mama? It's Amy."

"Amy? What's wrong? Shouldn't you be on your plane by now?"

"I think I'm going to be staying in New Zealand a little bit longer. In fact, I might be staying here for good. Mama, I'm in love. And I'm not sure what to do about it."

"Are you going to spend the day lounging about the house or do you want to come into the office and help me unpack my gear?"

Mal was stretched out on the leather sofa, his arm thrown over his head. "Nah, my leg has been sore. I think I'm going to hang out here."

"Dana told me about the girl," Rogan said. "That's why you were at the airport last night."

"Yeah," Mal said.

"Were you there to say goodbye or to convince her to stay?"

"Stay."

Rogan sat down on the arm of the sofa at Mal's feet, then rapped on the plaster cast. "You must have it bad."

"I don't," Mal said. "It's over. She left and there was nothing I could do to stop her."

"You could have grabbed her damn hand and told her you couldn't live without her."

"I kinda did that and it didn't work. Besides, what can I possibly offer her? You and Ryan probably don't remember how hard it was for Mum. When Dad would leave, she'd be so lost for days. Every time, it was as if someone had just flipped a switch inside of her and all the light would go out. I don't ever want to be the cause of something like that in another person."

A long silence grew between them. Rogan cursed beneath his breath. "So are we going to talk about them finding Dad or just pretend it never happened?"

"When did you hear?"

"When I got back to base camp everyone was gossiping about it. I couldn't get away from the chatter. There were reporters calling in, wanting to talk to me. Even in the middle of the Himalayas, they can get to you."

"Yeah, they can get to you," Mal murmured.

"Dana said this girl you're chasing is a reporter."

"Not technically. She works for *High Adventure*. Her father is Richard Engalls."

"Holy fuck, Mal. Dana didn't tell me that."

"I'm not sure she's aware. Or she hasn't made the connection."

"He funds some of the best expeditions out there. You don't think he'd—"

"No, I don't think he'd be interested in investing. Though he may want to fund an expedition. He's considering sending all three of us to Everest to recover Dad's effects. And they want to write about it in the magazine."

Rogan was stunned speechless, which was unusual since he was the talker of the family. "No," he finally said.

"That was my first answer, as well. But after talking with Amy over the past couple of weeks, I wonder if it might be good for us. Maybe we'd finally have answers. And it would stop Roger Innis from inserting himself into the story. If there's one guy more powerful in the mountaineering community than Roger, it's Richard Engalls."

"No," Rogan said, shaking his head. "I don't want to know."

"If we don't go, Innis will. He's after Dad's journal. He's worried there might be something in it that blames him for Dad's death."

"I don't care. Let our father rest in peace where he died. That's what I believe and I'll say that to the press. Besides, I don't think Mum would want it, either."

"She isn't happy about the idea, but she said she wouldn't stop us. Amy mentioned that we might want to consider doing a biography of Dad, and the idea is growing on me. Mum has all his journals. It might be a way to get to know him, the way we never could as kids. And a trip to Everest, to memorialize him, would be a fitting ending to the book."

"And who's going to run the business while all three of us traipse off to the Himalayas?" He glanced over at Mal. "Or do you want to do this for the girl? So she gets to write a big story."

"It's not like that. If we don't want to do the story, Amy is fine with that decision. And she won't write it without us."

"She could go to Innis," Roger said.

"She wouldn't do that. She cares about our family."

"If she cares so much, why did she leave?"

"It's complicated. I just couldn't give her what she needed."

"Which was?"

"I don't know. Stability. A man who actually spent time at home. How the hell are we supposed to make a relationship work when I'm gone ten months out of the year?"

"Maybe you ought to let her decide that." Rogan pointed out. "You forget, Mum and Dad loved each other. They chose to be together even though it was difficult. And how much different were we than any military family? Blokes in the navy are away for a lot longer than we are and they have marriages that survive."

"I asked her to stay and she didn't. What more am I supposed to do?"

"How did you ask?"

Mal shook his head. "I don't remember. I guess I

said, 'Will you stay?' and then I think she asked me why I wanted her to stay and I said because I didn't want her to go."

Rogan stared at him for a long moment. "That's it?"

"Yeah."

"You didn't say anything about how you feel?"

"That is how I feel," Mal replied, growing exasperated with Rogan's interrogation.

"Yeah, I would have left, too. Bloody hell, Mal, you have to give her more reason than that. You're asking her to give up her whole life back in the States to take up with you. You have to tell her what's in your heart."

"How come you're such an expert on this?"

"I watch Dr. Phil."

"Who the hell is Dr. Phil?"

"Some American shrink who has all the answers. We picked him up on motel television when we were doing prep for the McKinley climb. He's all about saying how you feel. So are you in love with this girl?"

"Yeah, I think I am."

"Why didn't you tell her before she left?"

"Because I really wasn't sure *until* she left. I was hoping she'd turn around and come back, but she didn't, so I guess it's just as well I didn't say anything."

"Crikey, Mal, you are as dumb as a bag of hair. She was waiting for *you* to say it. You were waiting for *her* to say it. It's no wonder you're sitting here without a woman."

Mal sat up and swung his broken ankle off the sofa. "What should I do?"

"You could always call her."

"She won't be home yet," he said. "I'll have to wait

until tonight. But 'I love you' is not something I should say over the phone. It would be better in person, don't you agree?"

"Yeah. It's always better in person."

"Then maybe I should go to her. I'm not working an expedition for a while. Now would be a perfect time. But what if the feelings aren't mutual and I go all that way for nothing?"

"You are a sad, sad case, Malcolm Quinn." Rogan stood up. "Come on, you're coming with me. We'll get some work done, take your mind off the girl."

"Nah, I'm just going to hang out here. Maybe have a beer or two, catch up on my sleep. You wanna get me a beer?"

"It's barely past noon," Rogan said.

"Liquid lunch." Mal pushed up from the sofa and hopped into the kitchen on one foot. He opened the fridge and examined the contents. There were all sorts of leftovers, meals that Amy had made in the days that they'd spent at home. Mal grabbed a beer and pulled out the spaghetti sauce.

He grabbed a spoon, then hopped back into the living room. As he made it to the sofa, a knock sounded on the door. "If that's Dana, tell her I don't need her to bring me any work."

Rogan stepped over to open the front door. He slowly stepped aside. "It's not Dana," he murmured.

Mal looked up and the sight took his breath away. Amy stood in the doorway.

"Hi," she said softly.

"Hi," he replied. "What are you doing here? I thought

you'd left. Why haven't you left? Was your flight cancelled?"

"Now would be a fine time to shut up and let the lady talk," Rogan muttered. "I think she's come here to say something."

"I—I have," Amy said. "Are you Mal's brother?"

Rogan held out his hand. "Rogan. I'm one of the twins. It's lovely to meet you. I've heard a lot about you. From Mal, of course. Talks about you constantly."

"Now would be a fine time for you to get the hell out of here," Mal said beneath his breath.

"Well, I have to go. Work to do." Rogan nodded at Amy as he walked by. The door slammed shut, leaving Mal to search for a way to begin the conversation. But Amy started it instead.

"I just came here to tell you one thing and then I'll leave. It may not make a difference, but it has to be said. I think I—"

"Love you," Mal finished. "I do. I think I love you. I wanted to say it at the hotel. And even earlier, here at the house. And on the mountain. But I wasn't quite sure how, it all seemed too complicated."

A slow smile curled her pretty mouth. "And now?"

"The moment you walked out of my life, I didn't know what to do with myself. I even followed you to the airport, but I couldn't get past security. I wanted to tell you that I need you, that I want you with me. And I know that it isn't going to be easy, but I believe we can make it work."

"I understand what your life is, Mal, and I understand how much it means to you. And I believe we can make it work, too," Amy said.

They stared at each other over the short distance, neither one of them daring to move. "Now would be a good time for me to kiss you," Mal murmured.

She nodded. But as he reached for his crutches, she crossed the room and threw herself into his arms. They both tumbled down onto the sofa in a tangle of limbs.

Mal's mouth found hers and he lost himself in a kiss that was both passion and promise. He'd never believed in love and had always thought it was for other people. But now he realized that he'd simply been waiting until the right person came along and made him see the light.

And here she was. His light in the darkness. His candle in the window. The one who'd always be there for him. Mal kissed her lips and then her cheeks and her nose and then her forehead. Amy giggled, her hands resting over his.

"What did you come here to say?" Mal asked.

"That I'm in love with you. We may have only known each other for a couple of weeks, but it feels like we were meant for each other. And I don't want to be apart from you. I want to stay here. I belong here."

"Where?"

"Here," she said with a smile, pushing him back into the sofa. Amy brushed a kiss across his lips. "I belong here."

"Yes, you do," Mal said. "And I don't ever want you to leave. That's an order."

"I don't have to follow your orders anymore. I'm not your client. I'm your girlfriend now. And that means that you have to follow my orders."

"And what would those be?" he asked.

Amy crawled off him and pulled him to his feet,

then handed him his crutches. "You need to go to your room. And when you get there, take all your clothes off and crawl into bed. And when I come in, I'm going to require some very careful attention."

"I like this new girlfriend thing," Mal said. "Is there anything else I can do for you?"

Amy nodded. "Just love me. And I'll be the happiest woman in the world."

Mal drew her into his arms and kissed her. That was one promise that was easy to make. He had everything he'd ever need in the world right here in front of him. And he had no intention of ever letting go.

Epilogue

Ireland, one month later

AILEEN QUINN STARED out the window of her country house, watching droplets of rain run down the hand-blown glass. Her mind wandered over the past year and all the changes in her life.

"Miss Quinn? Mr. Stephens is here."

She glanced over her shoulder to see her house-keeper, Sally, standing in the doorway.

"Would you like to see him here in the library or in the parlor?"

"Here," Aileen said, turning to walk to her desk. She leaned heavily on her cane. "And bring us tea, will you, Sally?"

"Yes, ma'am."

She and Ian had traveled a long road together, beginning when he'd worked for her as a researcher, preparing material for her autobiography. She'd hired him to find information about the family she'd never known.

Aileen had grown up in an orphanage. But her humble beginnings in life hadn't stopped her from becoming a successful novelist and one of the wealthiest women in Ireland.

None of that had made a difference, though, until she was able to track down her four older brothers who'd been scattered to the winds when their parents had died. Ian had painstakingly traced each one of them to a different part of the world—Australia, the U.S. and Canada. And then they'd found the last brother's heirs right here in Ireland.

Aileen had given each heir a sizable piece of her wealth, hoping that they'd use it in a way that might make a memory of her once she was gone. Though she'd never wanted to live to see a full century, she was quickly approaching that point.

"Miss Quinn?"

Aileen glanced up and smiled at the handsome young man who waited in the doorway. "I told you, you're to call me Aileen. We're friends now, you know."

"Aileen," Ian said, his usually serious demeanor breaking into a wide smile. "How are you?"

"Old," she teased. "I'd inquire about your well-being, but since I know you've just returned from your honeymoon, I needn't bother. You look tired, which I suppose is a good thing. How is Claire?"

"She's lovely. And she thanks you for the wedding gift."

"Yes, I got her note. I was hoping you'd bring her with you."

"She decided to finish out the school year before resigning. But I'm sure she'll stop by to talk to you about her new project. She's decided to write a novel."

"Well, I would be happy to give her some advice. I certainly have had enough experience at the job."

Sally arrived with the tea and set it on the corner of the desk. Aileen and Ian had shared the afternoon ritual so many times, she quickly made him a cup the way he preferred it, then put one of his favorite scones on a plate and held it out to him.

"I suppose you're wondering why I've called you here. Our work together has been finished for some time."

"I am curious," he said.

"There's been a new development in my search for my brother's heirs. And I thought I would give you the first chance to play detective before I hired someone new."

"I'd be honored to help you," Ian said. "But we found all four brothers."

She held out a file folder. "I received this letter a week ago from a woman in Auckland, New Zealand. She's been doing research on a family called Quinn and had watched Dex's documentary about my life. It sparked her memory of a birth record she'd come across."

Ian flipped the letter to the side to find a photocopy of an Australian birth certificate for a Lily Quinn, born seventy-five years ago. The parents listed on the birth certificate were Conal Quinn and Penelope Simpson. "Our Conal?" Ian asked.

"That's what I need you to find out. The birth year listed for him is a few years off, but the place is right. Cork, Ireland. And I've had another look at Conal's military record. He did spend a few years during the

Second World War in both Australia and New Zealand. He could be the father of this woman."

Ian scanned the letter. "It's a promising lead. I don't know how I missed it, though. I checked birth records in both Australia and New Zealand for listings of Conal Quinn as father after we received his military records."

"The way his name is written on the certificate it looks like Conor, not Conal. It was indexed wrong. I think it could be him. We were left wondering what had happened to him, assuming he might have taken on a new identity. Perhaps he went back to Australia or New Zealand after the war."

"Perhaps." Ian tucked the birth certificate back into the file folder. "I'll get right on this."

"Then you'll take the job?"

Ian smiled. "Of course I will. I will not rest until I find out the truth about this Lily Quinn."

Aileen clasped her hands together, tears swimming in her eyes. "I can't tell you how happy that makes me. I'm sure you'll do your best. And I'm hopeful that this clue might finally lead us to the whereabouts of my lost brother Conal."

Ian stood and came around the desk, then bent down beside her chair. "Don't worry. Now that we have this clue, maybe we'll finally know for sure. Maybe this Lily is still alive and she can tell us something."

Aileen reached out and took his hand, giving it a squeeze. "You really are a dear boy. And I'm glad you married into my family. My grandniece is quite lucky to have you."

"We're the lucky ones," Ian said. "And now that Claire and I are back in Ireland, we'll come for dinner some night soon. Dex and Marlie just got home from shooting a film in China, so I'm sure they'll want to tag along, too."

"The more the merrier," Aileen said.

She got to her feet, leaning heavily on her cane, then walked Ian out of the library to the front door. "I can't believe this is starting all over again," she said. "In all honesty, I'm rather excited. I've missed the intrigue. And now I suppose I'm going to have to call my publisher and add this to the next edition of my autobiography."

"I suppose you will," Ian said. "But if these leads result in another heir, you won't be too troubled, will you?"

"No," Aileen said. "After all, family is everything. I lived without a family for far too long not to want to know every last one of them."

Ian kissed her cheek, then walked to his car.

Sally joined Aileen at the door, hooking her arm through the older woman's. "Look how happy he is," she said. "I'm so glad he found his special someone. Has he decided to help, then?"

Aileen nodded. "The search begins again. Who can say where it might lead?"

* * * * *

REQUEST YOUR FREE BOOKS!
2 FREE NOVELS PLUS 2 FREE GIFTS!

red-hot reads!

YES! Please send me 2 FREE Harlequin® Blaze™ novels and my 2 FREE gifts (gifts are worth about $10). After receiving them, if I don't wish to receive any more books, I can return the shipping statement marked "cancel." If I don't cancel, I will receive 4 brand-new novels every month and be billed just $4.74 per book in the U.S. or $4.96 per book in Canada. That's a savings of at least 14% off the cover price. It's quite a bargain. Shipping and handling is just 50¢ per book in the U.S. and 75¢ per book in Canada.* I understand that accepting the 2 free books and gifts places me under no obligation to buy anything. I can always return a shipment and cancel at any time. Even if I never buy another book, the two free books and gifts are mine to keep forever.

150/350 HDN F4WC

Name _____ (PLEASE PRINT) _____

Address _____ Apt. # _____

City _____ State/Prov. _____ Zip/Postal Code _____

Signature (if under 18, a parent or guardian must sign)

Mail to the Harlequin® Reader Service:
IN U.S.A.: P.O. Box 1867, Buffalo, NY 14240-1867
IN CANADA: P.O. Box 609, Fort Erie, Ontario L2A 5X3

Want to try two free books from another line?
Call 1-800-873-8635 or visit www.ReaderService.com.

* Terms and prices subject to change without notice. Prices do not include applicable taxes. Sales tax applicable in N.Y. Canadian residents will be charged applicable taxes. Offer not valid in Quebec. This offer is limited to one order per household. Not valid for current subscribers to Harlequin Blaze books. All orders subject to credit approval. Credit or debit balances in a customer's account(s) may be offset by any other outstanding balance owed by or to the customer. Please allow 4 to 6 weeks for delivery. Offer available while quantities last.

Your Privacy—The Harlequin® Reader Service is committed to protecting your privacy. Our Privacy Policy is available online at www.ReaderService.com or upon request from the Harlequin Reader Service.

We make a portion of our mailing list available to reputable third parties that offer products we believe may interest you. If you prefer that we not exchange your name with third parties, or if you wish to clarify or modify your communication preferences, please visit us at www.ReaderService.com/consumerchoice or write to us at Harlequin Reader Service Preference Service, P.O. Box 9062, Buffalo, NY 14269. Include your complete name and address.

HB13R2

Double Take

Available May 2014 wherever
Harlequin books are sold.

Suddenly the ferry lurched again, making him glad for his
strong grip on the railing. But the woman—Lindsey—wobbled
on her feet and, for a second, he thought she'd fall. Not even
thinking about it, he stepped into her path and grabbed her
before she could stumble.

Their legs tangled, hips bumped and chests collided. He
had a chance to suck in a shocked—and pleased—breath,
when her fine red hair whipped across his face, bringing with
it a flowery fragrance that cut through the briny air and went
right to his head. Just like this woman was doing.

"Whoa," she murmured, either because of the stumbling
or the fact that so much of her was now touching so much
of him.

"I've got you," he said, placing a firm hand on her shoulder. He turned his back to the wind, staying close, but giving
her some distance and disengaging the more vulnerable parts
of their bodies. As nice as she had felt pressed against him, he
didn't want her to know that his lower half was ignoring his
brain's order to be a polite protector and was instead going

straight for horny man. Their new position removed the danger of sensual overload, but also kept her blocked from the worst of the wind. "I won't let you fall overboard. Now glove up."

Not taking no for an answer, he lifted one of her small, cold hands and shoved a glove on it. He forced himself to focus only on the fact that her lips now had a bluish tint, not that they were pretty damned kissable. And that her expression was pure misery, not that her face was shaped like a perfect heart, with high cheekbones and a pointy, stubborn little chin.

Once her hands were adequately protected, she stepped the tiniest bit closer, as if welcoming the shelter of his body. Mike heaved in a deep breath of cold lake air, but found it tasted of spicy-fragranced woman.

Nice. Very nice.

She licked her lips. "So you're single, too?"

He noticed she didn't add *available,* maybe because she didn't want to sound like she was interested, though he could tell she was; but he recognized desire when he saw it. During those few moments when she'd landed hard against him, heat had flared between them, instinctive and powerful.

"I'm *very* single."

Pick up DOUBLE TAKE by Leslie Kelly, available this May wherever you buy Harlequin® Blaze® books.

HBEXP79799

This unexpected hunk might be just what she needs!

According to his trading card, steady, marriage-minded—and gorgeous!—Max Dorset sounds tailor-made for Natalie Gellar. But when they meet, she realizes Max is only interested in a good time with no strings attached!

Don't miss the latest in the *It's Trading Men!* miniseries,

Seduce Me
by *Jo Leigh*

Available May 2014 wherever you buy Harlequin Blaze books.

Available now from the
It's Trading Men! miniseries by Jo Leigh:

Choose Me
Want Me
Have Me

Too hot to handle!

Jason Cooper broke Caroline Banks's young heart, and she's determined he won't get a second chance. But when the U.S. marshal strides back into her life looking hotter than ever, she wonders if her carefully guarded heart will be able to withstand the heat....

From the reader-favorite miniseries
The U.S. Marshals

Make Me Melt
by *Karen Foley*

Available May 2014 wherever you buy
Harlequin Blaze books.

Don't miss *Hard to Hold,* already available from
The U.S. Marshals by Karen Foley.

Ⓗ HARLEQUIN®
™

Blaze®

Red-Hot Reads
www.Harlequin.com

HB79801